LUNGA NOÉLIA IZATA

No Books Allowed

Ficha técnica/ Credits

Título/ Title

No Books Allowed

Autor/ Author

Lunga Noélia Izata

Editora/ Publisher

Publicação Independente / Independent Publishing

Capa/ Book Cover

Acácio Kavinda

Paginação/ Layout

Reedsy

Revisão/ Proofreading

Laura Joyce

Edição/ Edition

1ª Edição-Agosto 2024

(Edição em Inglês)/ 1st Edition-August 2024 (English edition)

Tiragem/ Printing volume

100

Depósito Legal/ Legal Deposit

13033/2024

ISBN

979 8334366206

Impressão/ Printing

Power Group print center

First edition

This book was professionally typeset on Reedsy.
Find out more at reedsy.com

In memory of
Kofi Selorm Sylvester Qweafi Azasoo
Heriberto Gomes
Adelaide Marília Vaal da silva

Contents

Preface

I missed you, Jodi...your voice...your thoughts. I think I did a good job in making you insane in your mind but so lucid outside of it. On the other hand, I poured all my angry thoughts into Adowa, and she embodied them. There is a saying, "I sat with my anger long enough until she told me her real name was grief." — C.S. Lewis. Adowa is the personification of this quote. I am not angry anymore; I have accepted my sorrow, and I hope Adowa does too.

I have something to tell you, Jodi. My dad is gone...it's been a while. I don't know if it gets easier with time or if we just accept it. Between me and you, it never gets better. Grief is like the "resting face syndrome," a facial expression that unintentionally creates the impression that the person is annoyed and irritated; it just becomes something that exists within us, and we can't control it.

Still, I tried to manage it by opening up to my imaginary friends, like you, Adowa, Gunda, Harlow, Mahamba and the like. Over time, I craved more than talking about my dad; I wanted to spend time with people who went through the same pain - who understood my suffering.

God gave me more than that. God gave me a job where I could

be there for others while healing myself. Working with urban refugees in Luanda, enlightened me and allowed me to see the aftermath of grief - the misery of losing everything and gathering the strength and passion to live.

I met humans forced to flee wars, persecution, violence, prejudice, and all types of conflict. The refugees saved me. They were not only forced to flee but also forced to grow and become self-reliant. Children were forced to become adults; to be away from their parents; to be there for their siblings; to teach themselves how to read; and still find joy in life. They were looking for protection; instead, they gave me everlasting inspiration.

No Books Allowed is a culmination of all the adventures I was fortunate to experience in this life so far, such as spending Christmas with friends from all over Africa; having lunch with African Ambassadors; publishing a book in Grahamstown, South Africa; discussing Climate Change with African feminists, in Accra, Ghana; writing poems in Brazzaville, Congo; riding motorbikes in the village of Wakiso, Uganda; watching "Chocolate com Pimenta" (Brazillian soap opera) dubbed in English in Kampala, Uganda; being stranded in Dakar, Senegal; enjoying food in Yaoundé, Cameroun; holding the phone of the Secretary General of the AfCFTA at his Swearing-in ceremony in Addis Abeba, Ethiopia; and spending the last days with my dad in Debre Zeyit, Ethiopia.

"Talk to the broken ones. They will teach you what is real, how to live alone. How to finish and how to start all over again." Sahil Verma

Acknowledgement

A special thanks to
  Laura Ellen Joyce
  Nair de Sousa
  Helga Silva
  Alister Chitetelee Pinto
  Salvador António

*References
  *"They Don't Care About Us" is a song by American singer and songwriter Michael Jackson, released in April 16, 1996, as the fifth single from his ninth album, HIStory: Past, Present and Future, Book I (1995).

*"When you pray for rain, you have to deal with the mud too." quote by Denzel Washington, actor (The Equalizer)

*"As Viúvas da Seca de Angola", documentary by VOA Português

Chapter 1

(Adowa)

I thought I already had faced my worst battles and lived through enough dark days. I had been promised freedom, and some sort of happiness, at the end of all this, but all this never ends. They expected me to be this brave woman who can endure all, but I was exhausted and scared. The cells were darker than the land on our side; the green of the forest illuminated our houses and we felt safe, at least for a while. The bars didn't give any sense privacy. I could see people in the other cell mourning, shivering and dying in a way that reminded me of how Vince described how the whites kept animals. I could feel the dust and smell it; it tasted like old sand. There was no furniture; we would lay on the floor and wait and wait till they would tell us what they were going to do with us. It wasn't really that different from life itself. I have been waiting all my life for a miracle, and hoping that things will get better, but nothing really gets better.

The floor was so cold that it reminded me of how Amina would sit on the floor to cool off when it was hot. Down here, the heat was boiling the bars, hot enough to cook my skin, so I stayed away from them. There was a little glimpse of light from the ceiling, but it wasn't enough to give me hope. I was done! I tried to sleep but it was unbearable with the background sound of people crying. I wanted to do the same. Why do people expect heroic people to not cry?

I spotted two guards accompanying a new inmate heading in my direction. As they approached, the sound of their footsteps made my breathing and heart rate increase; I didn't have a good feeling about this. They stopped at my cell and slid the bars open; the irritating noise gave me goosebumps. I saw that the man they brought was holding the Book.

"We have something for you," they said as they slid open the cell bars and pushed the man inside. That's all they said, nothing else – there was not usually a lot of talking here and I generally sat alone with my thoughts. They slid the bars back, closed my cell and left. I looked at my new cellmate. He looked physically tired, and his clothes were all crumpled. He was still at the door and seemed to be testing the waters with me before coming closer. I had the strange feeling that he knew me and didn't want to scare me.

"You brought the Book." I spoke first, pretending I wasn't frightened. That's the thing about being labelled insane: you pretend a lot so that they don't guess that you are startled.

"It´s for you." He approached me, slowly.

"Why? Who sent you?" I couldn't disguise my suspicious. I moved in his direction to receive the Book.

"A friend." He had a calm voice, not alarming.

He handed me the Book and started walking backwards, giving me space. He seemed to know I was uncomfortable with a man in my cell. As he moved, I could see the soles of his filthy feet; they were so dirty that I assumed he had been here for years.

2

This Book was black; it meant it came from someone who lived in Rhodesia during or after the revolution started by my comrade Jodi. She had made sure that the cover of the new Book would be black. The pages were cream and the letters black, just like my godchild. I leafed through the pages, trying to find something familiar. All I knew about the Book was that when you expressed a desire with intention THEY would hear you.

"The letters are too small ... I can't read them," I said while skimming through the book quickly.

"It's okay ... I can read it for you."

He treated me like he knew me. He wasn't scared of me like most people. I knew why people were scared of me: my facial expression was like a crystal ball that showed all the pain I had endured and my contempt for others. I wasn't sure how I felt about the suggestion, but something told me I could trust him. I handed him the Book and gave him a look that told him his proposal was granted.

He carefully sat down besides the bars, using them for support, not complaining about the heat. In fact, he seemed content to be there, like he had been waiting to be with me for a long time. I didn't know who this man was, but I thought I could trust him.

He began to read aloud. "I have fought the good fight, I have finished the race, I have kept the faith. Now there is in store for me the crown of righteousness, which THEY, the righteous Judge, will award to me on that day—and not only to me, but also to all who have longed for his appearing."

He had opened the Book randomly, but it seemed as though he wanted to specifically read that message. He didn't take a breath – it was as though he had been programmed to read that to me.

I kept observing him, wondering who he was and what this

3

encounter meant. He was dark, darker than me but with a different tone. I could never usually tell the difference between our colors – for me, all black people had the same tone – until I met him. Something about him was different, like he wasn't real. His skin was baby soft. I wanted to touch his face while he was reading but I didn't. His eyes were white and bright, and his voice was strong and held me under its influence.

In the deep silence of the cells, the verse echoed. I felt something powerful inside of me like hope disguised as faith or the other way around. Though I had never before read the Book in my life, I had been told from an early age that They were pursuing us.

"Do you believe in Them?" He spoke as he placed the Book on his lap.

"I believe in being alive ... in feeling things." I thought about our side of the land and all of us sitting down and listening to Amina. Back then I thought I believed in her, but throughout the years she became a different person, like power took over her. So, I made the decision to start believing in me. "I believe in you."

His caring eyes told me to trust him. He didn't reply, but his brief smile showed me that he understood.

"Why did you choose this particular verse?" I asked him instead of the other question on my mind. I thought about asking him who he was, but I choose not to. I didn't want to show that I was afraid.

"I didn't choose it ... I was talking about you. You fought the good fight and I know you have longed for me." He paused as though he expected me to say something. I was intrigued to see what he would say next. "I want you to know that you can trust me." he carefully slid himself along the floor to reach me and he leaned against me and placed my head on his shoulder. I didn't ask questions, I just obeyed him. I was still afraid but something inside me told me that there was nothing to worry about. I wasn't used to people not being afraid of me, so his behavior made me feel calm.

I fell asleep listening to his voice; it shut down my thoughts for a while. I slept tranquilly with no nightmares. Sometimes I wished I could sleep forever. I thought about death from time to time but a peaceful death, not the kind one where I was fighting for my life. I was tired of fighting.

I woke up feeling light on my face. There was a shaft of sunlight falling through one of the holes in the wall. I realized I was no longer leaning on the man; he had disappeared. Maybe I had dreamed of him? It seemed like a dream to find a man who wanted nothing from me.

The cell was mostly dark aside from the shaft of light. I inspected the whole cell until I saw something moving.

"Easy, easy ... I am here," he said, like he knew what I was thinking.

"What happened?"

"Nothing happened. You fell asleep, and I decided to continue reading but I didn't want to disturb you."

I looked around trying to understand if I was still dreaming or not. I knew the Elikyans didn't divide people into groups generally, but a man and woman in the same cell was a bit outrageous. Still, there was something serene about him.

"Do you want to go somewhere?" he asked, completely oblivious to the situation and where we were. I wondered what crime he had committed. He gave me his hand, and I followed him. He slowly opened the rusty door of the cell, and the noise woke up the men and women in the other cells.

It was the first time I had left the cell since I had entered it. I took everything in as we walked. Each cell had the same size and layout, and they were systematically organized. The guards stayed in square rooms with regular windows that only gave a view to the inside of the prison. The guards were as deprived of sunlight as we were. After passing the cells and the guards' rooms we reached a corridor that led to an open-plan room designed for the inmates to sit and socialize in and where there were circular grey seats where we could face each other and compare our crimes. We sat down and started looking around the place. There were wooden tables for people to play cards. Mirror had once tried to teach me a few games, but I told him that numbers were his mother's thing. The symbols of the cards reminded me of segregation. There was another more private area, where the reserved ones like me would sit.

I had taken a tour before but, with him, it was completely different. He painted a picture that the place wasn't as lifeless as it had seemed to me.

"What's your name?" I finally gained the courage to ask.

"Sylvester Kofi Azasoo."

He said it like he had lived a great life. I don't even remember my surname. They say that surnames can give us an outlook on a person's ancestry, history or their land.

"I like Kofi."

I smiled. I hadn't smiled in a while, and I had not had a conversation in a while.

"I want to show you around. There are days that guards let us rest there at night and look at the stars."

He pointed to an area where there was no ceiling. He seemed influential; if he had been a salesman he could have sold anything.

6

"What happened to you?"

I genuinely wanted to know. I didn't think this man was able to do any harm.

"I was a politician and I tried to expose those who betrayed the people."

He was straightforward and wasn't ashamed of what he had done. However, his eyes looked like he had endured a lot of pain.

"How can you still have hope?" I didn't want to enquire a lot about what he had done because I wasn't ready to share with him what I had done.

"I don't know how not to have hope."

He kept looking into my eyes, like he wanted me to inherit that same hope, but my heart was too shattered, for now.

I looked around trying to understand how he could pretend that everything was fine while he was locked in that place. The patio had walls with looser bars, not like the ones in our cells, wider, with more space between them, to give us an illusion that we were almost free. The white walls were dirty just like Kofi's clothes. He had definitely been here for years. I was afraid to ask more questions because I didn't want to spoil my intuition about him that he was good. The walls had handprints and impressions all over them; the dirtier the impressions were the more you could tell the gender and age of who had made them. Men and women, black and white, young people, and adults were all incarcerated here.

I looked around trying to understand what people did to end up here. What drove people to commit crimes? Was it jealousy, insecurity, insanity? I was familiar with the latter, but insanity only looks deranged from the outside – inside it can be more to do with conscience and discernment, and the burnout from carrying so many feelings.

7

Insecurity starts when you tell yourself you are less than others like what white people did to us. It didn't work; we didn't believe them. That's the key, to not believe them, to not feed into it. They say that when you show insecurity, people use it to humiliate you and it is deemed fair because you bring it on yourself by having a weak mind and thinking less of yourself. But the act of humiliating someone shows me that the predator might be the insecure one.

Jealousy starts unintentionally – a parent prefers one child unconsciously but shows it through their actions; the other child notices and develops an anger towards the sibling. The built-up angers turns into actions that affect the privileged child and they start a war internally and externally.

This solitude helped me organize my thoughts about every-thing. My internal voice changed – it became calm. I used to have angry thoughts – maybe this experience had humbled them.

"Adowa." He pronounced my name like he had known me for years. I wondered how he knew my name, but I wasn't completely shocked.

"Yes." I smiled, grateful to him for shutting down my thoughts.

"What is in your mind, dear?"

Dear ... Dear ... I don't think I was ever called that, but I liked being treated this way.

"I was thinking about life. How do we end up here."

I looked away, not facing him.

"This is not the end. It's the way and we will get out of here one day." He grabbed my hand and pressed it with his.

"I'm bit tired. Can we go back to the cell please?" I asked and started walking back. He obediently followed me.

8

The floor was hot, and my soles were begging for shoes. The guards had taken my shoes as though this ground was holy. They wanted to purposely humiliate us and force us to be vulnerable, or to completely lose ourselves. The more they exposed us, the more we felt we could be attacked or harmed. The secret was to never back down and to always carry ourselves like this didn't faze us.

I covered myself with the bits of clothes that I still had with me and shrank my body to protect myself from the night. He pushed me to his side so he could use both our bodies as pillows. I think we both fell asleep at the same time, like we were the same person.

In my dream, there was so much light, the kind of light I missed. The sun was out, and it didn't prefer either side, shining on black and white people. Nicola was walking seemingly happy, a shy happiness, the kind of happiness that comes all of the sudden even when your life is in despair. She was wearing a floral dress reinforcing that she was indeed happy. I couldn't see her face, but her essence told me she was okay. She kept walking and I couldn't tell if I was following her, or I was her in the dream. I then realized I wasn't in the dream; I was just the narrator, and I could see everything. I saw a black man driving a red car then I saw Theo's son whose name I couldn't remember but I knew him very well because Theo used to bring him to our side. He wanted him to be familiar with our race, culture and habits. In the dream, they all seemed happy. Mirror showed up and I could tell he was happy to see Nicola ... They all seemed happy... They all seemed happy.

"They all seemed happy," I whispered.

I woke up with a sense that I was losing my mind, a feeling which I had avoided since I arrived here. I tried to stay lucid so this cage wouldn't affect me. My body was concentrating blood flow to my brain; I felt lightheaded.

"It's okay. It's okay."

Kofi tried to rescue me from my delirium, but I was still disturbed.

"They all seemed happy." I continued to whisper the same but louder, trying to scream but the dream left me weak.

I tried to stand up, but Kofi pulled me down. I kept repeating my illusion like I was trying to convince myself, but I knew something was off.

"Yes. They are happy. Calm down."

He followed my thinking, without questions. He didn't care to ask who.

"Nicola was fine. Mirror was fine." I tried to calm myself down. I took a deep breath.

"Yes they are fine. Everything is okay."

He touched my face, trying to erase that memory. His palms features were similar to mine. I had this feeling that I knew him from somewhere.

I was getting used to waking up next to him but each morning I wasn't sure if he would be there; they could just decide to move him to another cell with no warning the same way they brought him here. There were no rules; the land of hope could do anything they wanted. Our side was known for being too strict and have rules or verses to control everything, but it gave us a sense of direction.

I was still shaking and trying to figure out if it had been a nightmare or just a dream. I had to go back to sleep to finish the dream or to forget about it. However, I was scared of waking up and Kofi being gone. Everyone always left, somehow.

I fell asleep again, but this time I had no recollections of any dream – maybe I didn't dream about anything, but I was told that every time we close our eyes we dream. I am always dreaming, even during the day: "daydreaming", that's what they call it, but it sounds happy, like you are thinking and manifesting good moments, but in my case, I was always thinking about the worst possible scenarios.

I woke up and he was literally next to me, like he knew I needed reassurance to avoid losing my mind. He had a very strong body odor – I couldn't decide if it was good or bad, but I could smell it strongly.

"Wake up, dear." He smiled and stood up, encouraging me to do the same.

"Let's move our bodies," he ordered. He stood up and jumped into a position with his legs spread and his arms raised. He paused, waiting for me to copy him.

I didn't move; I felt confused by this shift in energy.

"Adowa stand up ... now," he ordered me, gently.

I finally brought my moody self to his position and did what he was doing but with less energy and enthusiasm. While we were both exercising, I thought about the times I had enjoyed moving my body and dancing.

After finishing our exercise, he escorted me to the patio. I was breathing heavily, showing how stiff and unfit I was.

He laughed at how tired the exercises had made me.

Every time I was with him, I felt like there was music, like a background sound, like an instrument was playing next to us.

I also felt vulnerable, a feeling I had avoided since I arrived in this palace of guilt. Maybe the sound came from touching the metal bars or maybe when I met him there was some imaginary noise that I had automatically associated with him. Whatever it was, I felt safe.

"What are you thinking about?" He wanted to join me in my thoughts.

"Nothing. Just life."

I really wanted him to know that his presence made this experience bearable.

"Tell me about your life before this palace of guilt."

It's like he read my mind. I have been trying to read his, but I keep failing. I don't really read minds but people's energy and manners often revealed their plans before they opened their mouths. I didn't think I had a special gift until everyone in the black community started asking me to help them; they would take me everywhere and introduce me to everyone. The funny thing was that when it came to assessing people who would end up hurting me, I failed.

I drifted internally. I was eighteen again, beautiful, happy, bubbly... My body was toned, my shoulders were firm. It was as though THEY had made me perfectly able to withstand everything that was coming. My skin was young, and my tone was lighter. I guess that the dark days darkened my skin tone. Not that I cared or anything; I loved my tone but as the years went by I had started to notice that those details fueled by white people's agenda to provide reasons for us to hate ourselves.

I was walking around the green area. The wet grass reached my knees, I was wearing a red dress – red used to be my favorite color when I still favored anything. Do I sound resentful? Because resentment was the last thing on my mind. During those times there was nothing to resent, regret, nor people to avenge. I started running and then I threw myself onto the grass and I looked at the sky and I smiled. There was already separation during that time, but I didn't care. When you are young, you are naturally careless and selfish, adults criticize that trait, but with time, I envied my younger self.

The background music in my memories was similar to the tune I hear now when I am next to Kofi. I saw a white man, and the melody changed, the ambience became serious. I didn't care about them, but my people told me to not trust them. The man was older than me and full of himself, I could tell. I started reading people way before I got hurt; some people encounter their gifts by trauma, some are born with it.

"You shouldn't be here," he told me, as he approached.

He was a bit buff with strong legs and calves, stronger than mine. From an early age I was told I had beautiful legs and wide calves, but mine were nothing compared to his eggshell white, muscular, hairy calves.

"Says who?"

I wasn't asking for his name, nor did I fear this white man.

"Young lady, you need to go home."

"I always come here."

"I know but today is not a good day."

Had he been watching me?

"What happened?"

"One of you killed a white man."

"One of you?"

I could feel moisture gathering under my armpits.

"I am sorry. I just don't think it's safe. Okay?"

He blushed, which was commendable for a white person; they never usually cared how they came across.

I started walking back to our side.

"Wait. What's your name?" he asked, like there was more important information to be disclosed.

"Adowa," I obediently answered.

I was surprised I told him.

"Adowa, I don't think you should come here anymore."

He warned me like he cared, like he genuinely cared.

"What happened?"

"I told you a black man killed a white man."

He hesitated, trying to not offend me, like saying the word black in the wrong tone would be disrespectful.

"I heard you the first time. Where is the issue there? You guys kills us every day."

My tone was condescending. I wasn't embarrassed like he was, I had no compassion for them, but at the same time, no hate either.

"Just leave, please."

I started walking back to the black side.

I entered Armel's home. I sensed that something was going on the minute I entered the house. The feeling was probably also fueled by my strange encounter with the white man. The elders tried their best to protect us from learning unfortunate things, especially us women and kids. They didn't want us to be become enraged. We were just black people who lived happily ever after in our land, we knew nothing about being evil or anything. Our parents protected us so we could grow up with no traumas and lingering feelings. Except for Vince. Vince had inherited his anger from his father but at least he used it for good. Maybe that's why I fell in love with him, or I think I did. He was different from us – we were naïve and oblivious to everything around us, but not Vince. Vince being older and wiser was fully aware of the tension and the racial dynamics. And I was about to learn it all ...

"Where did they take him?" Armel asked Vince, walking around the room, impulsively.

"To the white prison below ground where they bury us alive. He is injured," Vince explained.

"Adowa will be home soon. We need to leave... She can't find out about this," he told Vince, while getting ready to leave.

I tried to hide myself, so they wouldn't notice me, but I wondered what they were keeping from me.

"Gunda should have waited for us. He shouldn't let his anger control him. This will be another reason for them to torture us. He will be used as an example."

Vince always sounded older, that's why I developed an infatuation towards him. Who was going to torture us? I wondered. Who would do something bad to us?

"Don't blame him. Grief changes you completely."

The more they talked, the more I was afraid of what I was going to find out.

"What happened?" I interrupted them.

"Gunda has been taken into custody. He killed a man."

Armel was practical; he didn't lie. I could tell from his voice that they didn't care about the crime; they were still going to be on his side.

"What's custody?"

"He is in prison. Listen, Adowa, you are a grown woman now. You need to understand everything. Things are going to change – we might go through some things."

He changed from the tone he was speaking to Vince, to a more a gentle tone.

15

"I saw a white man today." I felt like I had to confess. I knew my encounter wasn't random; something was going to change.

"Where? They will come here often, get used to it."

Vince never said a word, but I knew he was burping in the air 'I told you so'. Growing up, he used to tell me and the other kids those stories about segregation, and we all thought he was crazy, no one wanted to hang out with him, except me.

In time, I learned the whole picture. Years ago, the whites noticed the blacks' excellence in reading and writing, and they invited us to go to their side, to teach their kids. It had also benefited us. We had access to farms, and they gave us vegetables and fruits in exchange for our intelligence, but there was one condition, we needed to be vaccinated. I didn't know what the word meant until Vince kept going around telling people that the vaccines were faulty. The whites claimed that the injections were to protect us from any infections we would be exposed to on their side, since they had a completely different environment that we were not used to. Most of us believed them because they added that they didn't want to be responsible if something happened us, since we would definitely try to get revenge. I was very young then, but I remember not having a good feeling about that when they used the word 'protect' to lure us. The whites never cared for us to that extent, or to any extent at all.

First, the whites created hospitals, a place where you could seek help if you sick and we all laughed because we thought we could get any help we needed from our land, from the plants. When they mentioned the vaccines, we thought it was just another one of their crazy and dumb inventions. In reality, the vaccines were meant to control our anger, making sure that whenever we were on their side, we wouldn't retaliate. However, something much worse happened, something that not even the whites predicted. Some of the people vaccinated developed a condition that changed everything inside of them which still can't be explained. The doctors from their side and the healers from our side all had explanations but we didn't understand, we were just consumed by anger.

Gunda's father, one of the leaders of our community, contracted the illness. Elders say that Gunda's grandfather developed it first and Gunda's father inherited it. Others, consumed by anger and hatred of the whites, believed it was a side effect of the vaccine.

His father used to complain about pain in his bones, the swelling in his hands and feet, and he would often get sick. We started seeing more cases – some people were always tired and complaining about pain. It got so bad that we had to assess it and reach a conclusion. There were many gatherings during that time. I remember people shouting at the gatherings; I used to eavesdrop. I finally understood that a vaccine was something used to stimulate the body's strength and it was administered through a tiny needle.

While the elders met, Gunda's father was getting weaker. The elders would often invite Vince to join their gatherings – even though he was young, he was savvy and kept finding more information out about the issue. Conversely, they all hid this from Gunda. Gunda grew up a completely a normal kid, without that urge to be angry, until his father passed.

There was a white man at the entrance of one of the tunnels waiting for us with syringes and arranging us in a line. He would greet us every morning and repeat the rules of their side. When

Gunda found out what led to his father's demise he rushed to the tunnel and stabbed him several times with the syringes.

I don't think that man deserved that and that's when I realized this land was corrupt. He was just a servant, someone who was forced to do something, he didn't even know about the purpose of the injections. Gunda didn't have a plan; he was sobbing with hatred, and he just wanted to kill any of them so they could be even. I doubt Gunda felt any better when he had done this.

I wasn't anywhere near the scene, but I dreamed about it, and I had visions of the man's blood soaking the grass and the look of his dead eyes completely in shock, like he didn't know what he did to deserve this. His blood was just like ours and I wondered if maybe killing more white people to see their blood pouring out was the solution for us blacks to see that we were all the same.

I dreamed about that man for years, like he was begging me to avenge him, but I couldn't tell anyone about those dreams and feelings. I realized my own side was oppressing me. If I told them I didn't agree, I would be excluded. I think that's when I became insane, I couldn't find peace anywhere, anymore, until I met him.

I went back to that side, I wasn't looking for answers, I just wanted to be away from everyone. I sat on the grass, and it instantly turned red, the visions of that man lying on the floor confused tormented me. I started shaking my head like I was trying to wake from a nightmare. I felt a heat from my back and in my bones, I could feel his strong bones hugging me. I wanted to be hugged but I didn't know who he was. I looked back and I saw a peach-colored skin and cobalt blue eyes, which intrigued me. I had never seen eyes likes those.

"Calm down. Calm down." He kept hugging me. He didn't look disgusted by me, like I was told they felt.

"Don't touch me." I removed myself from the comforting hug.

"I'm sorry, I was trying to calm you down. Are you okay? I told you to not come this place again. I warned you."

He carefully distanced himself without seeming offended.

"This side does not belong to you."

I realized it was the same man from the last time, but I didn't even recognize him, they all looked the same to me. I remember seeing them as beautiful humans but not the kind of appreciation where you want to be like them, you just enjoy the view, but you are satisfied with your own looks.

"I know but I just don't want anything bad to happen to you." His voice was soft and caring, he instantly made me miss a relative or something. My parents were killed when I was young, and Armel raised me.

"Listen. Adowa. Go to your side. Things are not okay since ..."

He remembered my name and he pronounced it well. They always struggled to pronounce our names and I always found it funny when they tried while the others found it offensive. Vince got this name to enter the white side, no "traditional" names allowed. His real name meant 'evil'.

"Can you tell me what happened?"

"A man was killed."

This time he didn't mention races; it seemed as if he respected me, like he cared how I would feel.

"Why?"

"I don't know, and I don't think he knows why he was killed. I heard many stories."

It seemed the killing had really affected him. I understood him because I kept dreaming about the man too.

"I think he is okay now."

My recent dream told me that he was in peace with everything.

"What do you mean? You knew him?"

"No ... but I know he understands ... He is not resentful."

I wanted to offer my apologies on behalf of my people but that would be considered betrayal.

"How do you know all this, Adowa?"

His cobalt blue eyes changed to navy.

"I just know ... I know things ... I feel it. I have a question."

"Yes ..."

"Did he have a family?"

I was praying he would say no.

"He did ... a daughter ... a wife."

I touched my heart, but I had to move on from this.

"I am really sorry."

I almost cried but if I did I would have too much explaining to do. I would have to explain my dreams and how everything affected me.

"I know ... I can tell." He smiled. "They will be taken care of ... I will make sure of it."

I started wondering if he was close to the man, but I didn't dare to ask.

I kept going back to that place, completely ignoring his warnings. Sometimes I would find him and sometimes I wouldn't, but I always wondered who he was. He stopped asking me to not go there, instead, he revealed a lot of things to me. He shared that they were not scared of our anger, but they were scared of our diseases, which wasn't comforting to know but it was helpful. However, the injections were more like experiments, and they didn't care what the side effects would be.

They associated our dark complexions with dirt, and they assumed that because we worshiped land, mud, and soil we were not clean, and we carried diseases. I explained to him that our connection to earth saved us from multiple disease. I took pleasure in teaching a man something. Vince had told me that when he was being trained to be a teacher, they told him to not teach the kids about ecocide – which meant the destruction of nature by white man. Little did they know that we were dependent on our natural resources, and this allowed us to feed and protect our future generations.

I didn't understand what was happening, but I enjoyed being next to him. It was different from everything I had ever felt in my life. This man was everything I was told to hate – a man, white, and belonging to the white side.

One day, I placed my back against a tree so I wouldn't get tired from plaiting my coarse hair. Every braid made my arms weak, but I had to finish them. I enjoyed touching my scalp and feeling my hair; it was one of the best feelings. I could sense he was coming; this man was intrigued about me as much I was about him.

"You look beautiful," he confessed, looking at my hair.

I didn't respond, I just stopped braiding and looked at him. I usually had every answer on my tongue, but I hadn't been expecting this.

He sat next to me and pulled himself closer, not scared of my reaction. He touched my hair, and I felt his fingers gently sliding over my skull. I was disarmed. His fingers felt so good that I felt relaxed, and I forgot everything. If he had wanted to he could have killed me in that instant – he could have avenged his comrade in that moment. A life for a life, right?

He chose not to. Instead, he grabbed my face and touched my lips with his lips. I felt something warm in my mouth and I kept sucking and kept repeating it, I was not sure if I was doing it well, but I saw that his reaction to it was pleasant. He touched my feet and it felt like he was peeling off the plantar surface, and I smiled, the kind of smile that takes time to fade away – its traces linger in the eyes.

He looked surprised like he had never seen the body of a black woman before, but he wasn't going to stop. I was hairy everywhere, from my legs to my sideburns. I could feel his cold lips on my hairy legs, and it was as though his saliva smoothed every hair on my body and my angry hair behaved instead of being so rebellious. When he reached my face, he choose to kiss my cheeks instead of my lips. I didn't know what it meant but it felt good, like everything else. I thought whatever we were doing was done but there was more. He pulled my dress off while asking for permission with his eyes. How could you say no to blue eyes? He was perfect. I have never seen a white man naked, or any other man. He was also hairy, but his hair was obedient and yellowish, but light yellow like the gold men who lived in the mining areas. In the past, they were known for having a connection with the sun, the moon, or the stars, and treated with respect. Over the years they had been largely shunned, hunted down, mutilated, murdered, and accused of making muti in witchcraft. They had been dragged out of their lands and found rescued in Elikya.

I wanted to do to him the same thing he was doing to me, but I didn't know if it was acceptable. I didn't know what a woman was supposed to do. Were we supposed to do this? Was this love?

"I love you."

I think he read my mind. That sentence unlocked everything in my precious body. My back was still leaning against the tree, so he pushed down my whole body and I felt the sand scratching my back. I had dirt all over me, but he didn't care; he didn't seem grossed out. Instead, he looked amazed by my body. He kept moving me from side to side, he knew all the rules and I just followed. He knew exactly what he was doing. It felt like he wanted me to feel good, like somehow, I deserved this.

You know how the brain is in the command and tells the body to move, this time my body took over because my brain wasn't really functioning. Like the body moved first and then the brain noticed, and it was shocked with my body's power. Things started rough and fast and with time they became slow and gentle. Is it possible to need something we didn't even know existed?

My breath calmed and my whole body rested. He sat down next to the tree and placed my body in between his legs.

"I have never done this." I breathed slowly and confessed it. Any woman, from any land, always has this feeling that urges us them to let the man know we are pure.

"I know. Me neither."

He didn't seem to care, and I didn't understand what he meant because he was older than me and he looked experienced. Maybe he meant he never done with a black woman before. But the truth is we had been intimate since the first time we saw each other. It felt like our bodies were meant to be together, like iron influenced by a magnet. I had tried to fight it, but I kept coming here, ignoring all the black voices in my head.

He kissed my head from the back.

"I need to go ... They are probably looking for me."

"When am I going to see you again?"

"I don't know. I am not sure."

I was about to end whatever this was.

"Let's run away," he said, peacefully and certainly.

"Hmm ... What do you mean?"

23

I had to pretend I didn't like the idea, but I did. There was not much here for me. My parents were gone and all I had was myself.

"I don't know ... Let's go somewhere far ... So we can be together."

He turned my face to his and smiled.

I was on top of Kofi now, moving my body, and he was just staring at me, like I was the one in charge. The cells were darker than us, so dark that no one could see us. His whole body had a dark complexion. Some people have a dark face and a light body, but he was dark from head to toe. Perfectly dark, no different tones or anything. He was so dark that you couldn't see any blemishes or marks. I could feel his gluteus; he was toned, and I felt resistance. It made hard for me to move properly. I wanted to give up because I wasn't recreating the scene in my head. It wasn't the same ... He wasn't white ... He wasn't mine ... He was obedient to my movements and didn't dare to say a word, like this was all about me and whatever I wanted. I wanted to feel exactly how I felt years ago between the trees. His smell was different, everything about him was different. He wasn't him. I removed myself from on top of him and rested on the floor.

"What happened to him?"

He carefully dressed and begged me to continue my story.

"He disappeared."

I smiled to avoid remembering what had happened.

"I was rooting for you."

What did that mean? He didn't know me back then.

"Me too. But I guess it wasn't meant to be." A tear fell down my cheek and Kofi wiped it away.

24

"It was ... Everything is meant to be ..." He said it like he knew exactly what happened to the white man.

"For weeks, I went to our spot waiting for him and there was no sign of him ... I thought he changed his mind or something ... maybe thinking that he changed his mind was better than facing the reality that he was gone."

"I am sorry." Kofi expressed his compassion, but I doubted he would have the same sentiment for what I was about to reveal.

"The weeks turned to months, and I realized I felt different ... I knew love could give you a completely new perspective on life but something inside of me was growing." I smiled remembering when I found out.

Kofi also smiled, thinking there was a happy ending for this.

"I was pregnant ... with a mixed child ... a son of a white man and a black woman." I chose my words carefully to make him understand why I had to do it. "He was growing and growing, and people started noticing ... I had heard stories of what whites did to the mixed babies ... if they could kill their own, imagine someone who wasn't entirely white, just partial, just a little bit ... with a little bit of black blood." I wanted to throw up, thinking about what I did to my own, my own blood. I couldn't bear explaining what happened.

Kofi hugged me.

"For years, I thought I deserved a punishment for what I did but I didn't realize I was living a punishment itself ... killing my own baby, not having the opportunity to take care of him was more than punishment ... these cells, bars ... are nothing compared to what I lived all these years."

My shoulders dropped and my usual headache started to kick in.

"And whoever exalts himself will be humbled, and he who

humbles himself will be exalted." Kofi professed the verse with a singing voice, without relying on the Book; he knew every verse. His voice caressed my thoughts.

"I used to hear this at every trial, and I thought it meant that we would be free from anything or honored at the end ... but I came to realize it's about being content with life ... finding joy in humility."

I never sounded so sane.

He was in silence for a while, grasping everything and choosing his words carefully to fully be there for me.

"What was his name?"

"I don't know... He never told me..." My mind froze on his face, on his blue eyes and tiny mouth, with no lips. I realized loving was so easy, it wasn't these mix of battles that everyone were talking about.

"No ... I mean ... Your baby..."

"I can't remember ... I think I had a name, but it got lost in my mind ..."

Chapter 2

(Jodi)

I couldn't stop thinking about her. Adowa, Mirror and Aunt Noli were the only family I had. That place would slowly kill her.

I regretted coming here, I shouldn't have, I should just have accepted my son the way he was. I was so committed to proving that he wasn't a crime that I didn't realize that he was perfect the way he was.

I sat at the porch of Harlow's house, holding the Book, but the moment I saw her I hid it. A voice told me to hide it.

"What do you have there?" She noticed it.

"It's the Book." I showed it to her.

"I don't think I've ever seen one, but we need get rid of it. Mahamba forbids the people from reading. Only the leaders can read."

What? What kind of land was this? I had so many questions.

"Tell me more about the leaders please," I asked, completely disturbed by what I just heard.

"We will meet them tomorrow. There are eighteen of them and they are in charge of protection our land, making sure everything is transparent and impartial. They are not related ... They are just people who have seen a lot in this land who can counsel us and decide our fate. They are the land's memory and legacy. They are eighteen completely different people from different tribes and families. It's our way of ensuring fairness."

She sat next to me as she explained.

"I see but tell me about the trial. How can I find a good lawyer for her?"

"We don't have lawyers here. There is no such a thing as a profession. We are just living."

She sounded like she was bored with everything and didn't agree with my concerns.

"I don't understand. So, what do you guys do the whole day?"

Taking care of Mirror was my full-time occupation but before all that, I had dreams and I had wanted to do something.

"Jodi, there is a lot that you don't know about this land ... and you will soon understand, but please have hope for Adowa."

"I can't stop thinking about her."

I was panicking but I had to be strong for Adowa.

"Don't worry, she is fine, she is strong, she is probably managing."

Did Harlow know her? I wondered. I thought that these people knew more than they said they did.

"People who have been through abuse lose their sense of reality, you can never trust what they say, they create a parallel world in their minds to survive. They truly believe something didn't happen just to protect themselves from the pain, trauma and the memory. They will say one thing and then say they never said it because they play characters. They were taught to never be themselves because being themselves led to constant abuse."

I thought about Adowa and imagined her frightened in there.

I asked Harlow if we could somehow send the Book to Adowa, since prison was considered the land of lost souls, and no one cared what they were doing there.

She arranged a room for me to stay. She was being very helpful considering the fact I came here to investigate her like she was a deficient human. The room was wide with a bed in the corner, covered with a with a red fly net. There were holes in the net which meant the insects here were fighters. I had been told stories about the red flies and the different ways they emerged, but I was not too apprehensive about them. I guessed they were prevalent here. I opened the net and lay in the bed. I left it a little open; I didn't believe in red flies. A part of me was still very much white and believed I was immune to it.

The next morning, Harlow woke me up and took me to the house of the leaders. Mahamba was waiting for us at the entrance. I was still not sure about his role in the land – who was he really? What power or leadership was under his belt? The house was a townhouse with a rooftop that you could see from afar. We entered a room with a very hot atmosphere which led us to another room filled with broken, old sewing machines. I thought about Aunt Noli. I wondered how she was managing with Mirror. There were many rooms in the house with dust and spiders everywhere; everything looked old and forgotten. The windows had bars making them almost impossible to open. It seemed like the house was an old prison cell.

They escorted us upstairs; the stairs were slippery and very narrowed; most black women from Rhodesia with their volup-tuous figures wouldn't be able to pass. On every floor there were rooms that seemed oddly empty. Like technical or vocational rooms that were supposed to be used for something specific but had been abandoned.

From the rooftop, you could view the whole land. There were eighteen men, women, and even children, sitting in a circle on white, wooden chairs. The whole set up felt judgy. They had left three empty chairs for us, and they introduced themselves.

"My name is Benguela, and I am here to hear the case of your loved one." She was a beautiful light-skinned woman who looked like a perfect combination of black and white and seemed compassionate.

"My name is Luanda. We are here to serve you. We are happy to host Rhodesians." He was politely fake. His head was big, and it seemed like it wasn't in harmony with his neck.

"I am Cabinda." He had a different tone, like he was a mixture of Amina's spices. His hands were darker than his face.

"I am Bié." His accent was different.

"I am Bengo." She was a dark-skinned, chubby woman who looked like she would sympathize with Adowa's situation.

"I am Lunda-Sul." She was a long, slim, but curvy woman; you could tell she was a certain age, but her skin didn't reveal that.

"I am Lunda-Norte." She was angry with her words, like she didn't want to be there, like she didn't believe in the system. I would remember her because of her curly hairstyle.

"I am Kuanza Norte." She was a voluptuous women who looked familiar.

"I am Kuanza Sul." Another woman, whose eyes reminded of Adowa. I sensed the land really empowered women. Perhaps their fight wasn't black vs white, it was women vs men.

"I am Namibe." A young, black man who seemed confused.

"I am Uige." Another black man who smelled like dark plants.

"I am Zaire ... This unique case of this lady has come to our attention." He was an erudite white man: you could tell from the way he choose his words carefully.

"I am Huila." Another black woman, who stuttered.

"I am Huambo." A white man who seemed uptight and would be hard to convince that Adowa deserved freedom.

"I am Cuando-Cubango." A young man. When I looked more closely, he seemed very young, in fact. I wondered what impact he would have in the case.

I also wondered what all these names meant.

"I am Cunene." An older man who reminded me of the elders from the black side.

"I am Malanje." A woman who presented herself in a language that I couldn't understand but resembled sounds I used to hear on the black side.

"I am Moxico." A young girl, with a brownish and reddish skin tone, with long dark hair, introduced herself.

They went around in order until they reached the last person who was sitting next to me. I then heard a voice coming from my right.

"Jodi ... these are the eighteen counselors of this land ... We shall have no others before them ... They guide and protect us. We also use the forest to protect us ... to make sure we know the intentions of people who come here." It was Mahamba who explained this.

It felt like I heard this all before – a perfect system that didn't work. Everything seemed rehearsed.

I spoke. "Adowa's intentions were not to cause any harm, just to accompany me." I felt like we were already on trial.

"We understand that, Jodi, but she committed a crime before

coming here and that says a lot about her character."

Mahamba's voice was so serious that I was afraid Adowa would never leave this place.

"What crime did she commit please? I still haven't understood this," I humbly asked with the politest tone I could find within me, even though I was boiling inside.

"It has come to our attention that Adowa killed her son."

What? How could they know? Did she tell somebody else? I wasn't sure if I should lie or pretend that I didn't know what he was talking about.

"What son? Adowa does not have any son."

I tried to control myself. I closed my fist, and I eased my mind, telling myself I wasn't lying. I realized they had mentioned the forest earlier and then I thought about our conversation there. Had someone been listening to it?

"Jodi ... Adowa had a son years ago and she assassinated him."

Mahamba was firm and it was clear that he didn't have time for any nonsense. His tone was scary.

"Yes, it's true. She confessed to me, but it was years ago in our land ... I don't understand the jurisdiction here."

I crossed my legs to show that I knew what I was talking about. Sometimes we don't realize how many years have gone by and how much we have grown until we need to rely on that growth.

"Listen. Was she prosecuted in your land?" His arrogance was obvious. He knew she wasn't.

"No ... But ..."

"So, she needs to answer for her crimes," he interrupted.

"I don't consider it a crime. She did it because the whites were going to kill her son anyway." They didn't care about skin tone, but they were all looking at me pointing out with their eyes that I was a white woman.

"This is not about you Jodi. This is about maintaining the peace of our land," he said, calmly, not being aggravated by how angry I was getting. It's not the first time he had indicated that he thought I was of full myself.

"What evidence do you have?"

I completely disregard his attempt to bribe me with the anthem of the land.

He stood up and started walking to the fence, where you could see the sweep of the land. He made a gesture for me to follow him.

"You see the forest – our Caputo?"

He showed me like he was some kind of nobleman and proud of his so-called land of hope. I could tell there was something about the forest, it was different, it was so dry, drier-than-normal conditions. It looked like it has been like this for years. I don't know what this effect meant but I wondered what it had to do with Adowa.

"Our Caputo might not be an attractive plantation ... perhaps the lack of plantation gives visitors the impression that it is a meaningless forest, but it has a great deal of importance for us Elikyans." He spoke with a naughty smile.

I was silent. I didn't want to interrupt him; sometimes egocentric people lie on themselves and expose themselves. I looked over to Harlow, asking for help to try to understand this man and this land.

"I see, we spent a night there, we didn't do anything ... any harm." I tried to remember that night.

"I know, we saw you, we heard you."

Everything about his words alarmed me.

"What do you mean you heard us?" I wasn't being polite anymore, I didn't care.

33

"The trees can hear you, each of us here can hear exchanges taking place in Caputo. You see, we were given this gift, and it allows us to protect our people them from any harm."

As he talked, I looked over to every leader, trying to see if they all agreed. Over the years I had come to realize that people imposing rules always want you to believe that there was a higher power who selected them, that they were chosen to do this.

"We receive everyone, we welcome everyone, we only have one condition – we want to know your intentions." He spoke slowly, like he was spelling each word.

"You come, you confess what's in your heart, we listen to you, and if there is indeed a crime that has been committed we hold a Babemba where we give this person another chance to explain themselves. And then the eighteen leaders will rule!"

That yearning to judge others gave me goosebumps – it was the same greed that drove my father crazy.

"It seems fair but eighteen is an even number. What if...?" I looked over to the leaders, knowing I couldn't memorize any names or faces.

"If the leaders don't reach a conclusion, I will rule." It appears he had already decided Adowa's fate.

"Are there any lawyers? People to help?" I thought about Harlow's warnings. I hoped he was going to give me good news.

"No. Adowa's fate is in the hands of the leaders."

"How can I prepare her defense?"

"The leaders will discuss it."

"Will they use the Book?"

Harlow gave me a look.

"What Book?"

"The Book, you know."

I was choked that they didn't know of the Book.

He looked over to the other leaders and made a sign, translating that this conversation was getting out of hand, but he kept his demeanor at ease.

"We rely on ourselves only, on discipline, on lessons and on the different stories of the people we welcome into our land. I am aware that the Book wasn't a success in Rhodesia."

He started walking around, with his face down, hiding his snarky smile. He couldn't camouflage that he was proud of how their land was established.

"I was told it was an attempt from certain people to trick you."

He meant white people, but Elikyans didn't make separations.

"Yes, but it became our salvation. It helps us." I said it proudly.

"I don't think it really helped you, mam." It was getting clearer that he wasn't proud of my accomplishments or attempts to help my friend.

"So, is there any source of information, something I can read ... What do you rely on? How do you make decisions?" I was asking but without making fun of their system.

"Intuition ... We rely one our senses, how we feel about things ... I am sure you being a strong woman can testify to this."

I had a feeling he knew about my dreams.

"I understand but books can better our sense, our common sense ... What about education?" I looked at the two adolescents who were part of the leaders group.

"No, you people started everything with this education, colonization, racism, etc. You read these things in the books ... You started this whole thing ... We want to protect our people ... books are distractions, and I would appreciate it if you wouldn't mention them again." He crossed both his arms behind him and started walking back to his seat. He didn't want to talk anymore.

There was a deep silence, and I rested my case.

Harlow escorted me back to the house. I was still processing this thing about them listening to people and trying to figure out how I was going to get Adowa out of this land. On the way, I looked around trying to understand every piece of this land. The houses were all the same height, next to each other; it seemed as though they lived in confinement, where there was no privacy to instigate *a coup d'etat.*

The houses looked like shacks and there was brownish sand everywhere, it would instantly make you dirty. On the white side, we had pavemented floors, and on the black side there was grass everywhere. I missed walking barefoot and feeling every bad thing leaving my organism. The black side was therapeutic for me in many ways, and I made sure Mirror experienced it.

I spoke aloud to Harlow. I knew I could trust her. I didn't think coming here had been a mistake.

"Is there a way I can help my friend?"

"Yes, there is."

"That place will destroy her. We need to get her out."

"There is someone who can helps us," she said while opening the door of the house. She seemed like she was waiting for someone to enter the house, like there was someone following us on our way back.

Benguela appeared behind us, carrying something heavy in a cloth bag. She was one of the few I remembered because she was unforgettably beautiful.

"I am sorry. We had another meeting after you guys left. Here, I brought you some books that you guys can read about women

36

who decided to interrupt their own pregnancy ... some are diaries of women from different lands ... others are recollection of events told by people who were touched by their stories." She placed the books on the table.

I had some questions. I thought books were not allowed.

"So, people have done it before?"

"Yes, a lot of them ... Some didn't survive to tell the story ... Some don't want to tell their story."

"This is very common, especially when someone is expecting a mixed child," Harlow added.

"But I thought you were okay with this ... that Elikya was open to everyone."

I was trying to understand this land, but this system of liberation was more confusing than our segregation.

"Yes, we are okay with that, but I am talking about women who run away from their own lands and come here for sanctuary. I have heard many stories ... Some didn't arrive in the best shape ... I wondered what Adowa went through ... She must be very strong. I want you to be strong for her. Listen Jodi, you asked if there is something you could do for her ... Yes, there is. Not everyone is brave enough and might suffer the consequences, but I don't think you have anything to lose."

It seemed like she was waiting for this, for someone to confront the leaders. I thought about Mirror, I had to go back but I couldn't leave Adowa behind, especially in this situation – she came here for me.

"So, when the Babemba starts, people will be gathered around Caputo watching everything, but not within the trees, they will be around, not inside. The leaders will be in one side and the people in the other side. Adowa will be brought in to explain her crime and take responsibility. The leaders will listen to her carefully and talk amongst each other then they will ask if someone has anything to contribute to her fate. Most people stay silent because they can't even make proper sentences. They are not clever, bright, or courageous enough. So, you will intervene and fight for your friend," Benguela finished, explaining her plan, smiling. She used the table to show me where people stand and the leaders' positions in the forest.

"Initially, a Babemba was to forgive people and embrace them. When someone did something wrong, we would make a circle, put the person in the center of Caputo and start remembering all the good things they've done in their lives. We would speak highly of them. The influence of Caputo would make us say even more beautiful things. As time went by, we misused its grace. It wasn't about welcoming people shortcomings anymore – it was about exposing them."

I could tell how nostalgic this was for her.

"What's in it for you?"

I knew I could trust Harlow, but I had to know more about Benguela.

"I feel for Adowa. I heard about her before you came and when we all listened to your conversation in Caputo, I felt that I should help. She didn't have an option. She had to do it ... maybe today she wouldn't have to and that's why we fight so the women in the future won't be in this situation or won't be judged by it."

I was convinced. I had no more questions.

Later, Harlow explained that long time ago Benguela was raped, got pregnant and contracted a virus that attacks the body's immune system. She was told the baby wouldn't survive, so she chose her fate. The leaders persecuted her, she fought, and later was asked to join the group. Vince used to say that the people in the power were once victims or rebels who wanted change. His voice lingered in me.

I spent weeks reading the books and protecting them. Whenever someone came to check on us, Harlow would tell me to hide them. I read a story about a woman who was raped by different men at the same time, her name was Florence. I could feel her pain through her words but listening to her I could tell that the experience didn't break her. There was another story about a woman who was pregnant, and her husband's ex-wife threw hot boiling water on her belly with the hopes of her losing the baby. I wondered what drove people to that extent of hate. Are men worth it? Well, I mean I left my family and people for one man.

Each of the women's stories reminded me of the pages of the book I wrote years ago. I also thought about Dad. I never told anyone this, and I am glad Caputo didn't influence me to say this. I went to see my dad in prison after Vince died. I wasn't incensed nor indignant, I just wanted him to meet his grandchild. He refused. I can't say I was surprised or shocked, but I realized everything in that moment. My dad didn't hate black people, he envied them. When you see a community of people content with whatever they have, even though you did all you could to destroy them, it infuriates you. You start looking for flaws to justify your anger. There was no basis for these trivial annoyances, they were used to justify killing many people.

The leaders set a date for the Babemba, and we waited. I

wondered how she was coping. I wondered if she had kept the baby whether tings would have worked out just like people learned to accept Mirror. One thing about Adowa's character that always impressed me was that she was never envious or resentful towards me for being able to have a mixed son. She loved my son like he was hers.

Harlow accompanied me to escort Adowa from the prison to Caputo. I was told I couldn't visit her, so I didn't know if she was skinnier, bigger, or angrier. I saw her from afar, and we walked towards her. She looked fine, which was alarming because how could you be okay in that situation? She kept asking the guards for someone named Kofi and they all ignored her. Who was Kofi?

In Caputo, all eighteen leaders and Mahamba stood around the trees and we the people from Elikya stood on the other side, allowing Adowa to be in the center, alone. I wondered if they told her how this thing was going to go.

It was so dry. There were leaves on the ground, everywhere, more than on the actual trees. Harlow shared that she believed that the darker the secret the more the trees died. The trees were tall and completely naked and couldn't hide the power of the sun, lingering on Adowa 's dark skin. The sun was reflecting in her eyes, and she was struggling to see us.

I started inspecting the forest trying to understand it. All my life, I knew these things existed, especially moving to the dark side, but I always wanted to understand them, just like I have tried all these years to understand my dreams. Ironically, recently my dreams had stopped. At first, I had felt at ease because I was always anxious before going to sleep but now not knowing was also making me fearful, for everything.

"We are gathered today to welcome Adowa to our land."

40

Mahamba started the session.

Harlow explained that the rationale was to assess someone in order to welcome them to Elikya, so if they were cleared from any accusations, they would be invited to live in Elikya.

"My name is Mahamba, I am the main leader of Elikya ... The land of hope. Years ago, we decided to create a way to protect our land from ill-intentioned guests."

I wondered if Adowa was aware of Caputo and everything that came with it.

"I want to introduce you the leaders ... Luanda, Cabinda, Bie, Bengo, Lunda-Sul, Lunda-Norte, Kuanza Norte, Kuanza Sul, Namibe, Benguela, Uige, Zaire, Huila, Huambo, Cuando-Cubango, Cunene, Malanje and Moxico ... They are all here for you."

They all made a gesture to introduce themselves. They were all wearing long gowns of different colours; old and fusty. Adowa didn't even look at them. I had a feeling she was confident about this; I don't know how she managed to survive yet another battle. This woman was something else.

"Adowa please tell us why you are here." Mahamba finished his introduction.

"My name is Adowa. I am from Rhodesia. Years ago, I had a son with a white man and out of fear I killed my son." She stood strong, and unapologetically explained. I was expecting Adowa to say something like 'I don't know, you brought me here', but she was calm and collected.

Mahamba first looked at the others and then asked, "Okay. Have you regretted your actions?"

"Yes. I have ... Every single day."

"Okay ... I see ... I will discuss the matter with the leaders, and we will rule your fate."

41

He was ready to step away and walk with the leaders, when Adowa stopped them.

"I have more to say."

She grabbed her fist like she was ready to fight physically. I didn't know what was behind this transformation, but I was loving it.

"Yes ... Please ... We would like to hear."

He had a fake tone that didn't give any comfort at all.

The dreams were gone but my intuition was strong, I knew he was the ill-intentioned guest. When someone constantly tries to expose people, they are hiding something themselves.

"I was born in a land where everything was separated ... divided. But I found love in this separation ... It was the strongest thing I ever felt in my life. And this love became stronger when I felt it inside of me ... I can't remember many things because a lot has happened to me that I don't know who I am anymore ... I don't know if I am strong ... If I am weak ... I just know that I am tired ... I am tired of being angry ... I am trying to fighting ... I am just tired."

Her voice seemed as she was going to collapse, even though she said she didn't remember a lot of things, I think the thoughts violated her while she was speaking. I don't know if Adowa was the strongest or the weakest person, I know but she was a good person, and she didn't deserve this.

Harlow was silent the whole time, but she looked impressed.

We were tired; it was a long time to be standing. The people looked hungry like they hadn't eaten for days.

I caught Harlow looking at people from time to time, she really cared for them.

"The earth ... Rhodesia ... Elikya ... is our garbage, we throw away our emotions and some people get hit by them ... I was hit too many times."

I wondered if she had been influenced by a mystical power? I wanted to intervene, to help her but Harlow stopped me. I wondered how come that day when Adowa poured out her heart, I didn't reveal that I missed being a white girl with parents and a sister.

"I paid the price already ... Mukhonda? Why do I deserve this? I will accept any fate ... sentence you decide but there is no harsher sentence than living without my son." She took a deep breath.

Mukhonda ... Mukhonda ... I kept repeating very low ... I remember this conversation with Vince, where he told me that sometimes there's is no answer to why. I just couldn't understand it. Mukhonda ... I missed home. I never became fluent in the black side lingo, but I understood a bit.

She wasn't done. The whole crowed gasped like they never seen no one so outspoken and so broken.

"I was going to call him Monami ... I didn't have a chance ... but I see him in my dreams all the time ... so I am thankful for that."

Then she was silent. We weren't sure if she was done but there was no way the leaders wouldn't let her go after this. The leaders stepped away and you could tell that Mahamba wasn't pleased, especially seeing the reaction of Elikyans. They started cheering for Adowa. I was amongst them, but I couldn't understand their language.

By the leaders' demeanors and Mahamba's expression, the decision wouldn't be unanimous. At least half of the leaders were touched. Benguela later revealed to us that most of the women faced Mahamba and told him that if he cared about women, he would let her go.

They started walking back, Mahamba wasn't pleased; he wasn't asked to rule the Babemba.

"We heard your story carefully and we are obliged to welcome you to our land ... We all agree that if Elikya is the land of hope, we must be compassionate to your story and bravery ... We apologize for anything you have been through, and we hope your stay here will ease your pain in any way possible."

Cabinda ruled. The show was over. I couldn't hear him properly but whatever he said, it meant that Adowa was free to go. The trees around us looked happier. Adowa collapsed on the ground, and I rushed to her rescue. Was this the end?

Chapter 3

We woke up with the noise of someone knocking on the door. It was Mahamba with his faithful leaders inviting us to see the land. We got ready and respectfully joined them. Harlow was told not to come, which was alarming. I hope I didn't bring trouble to her. I was once told that everywhere I go I brought trouble. Was I the Adowa of the whites?

There was sand and dust everywhere and our clothes became instantly dirty. My first weeks here, I spent most of the time inside of Harlow's house. This thing of the forest hearing us and knowing our secrets didn't sit well with me. I wasn't afraid of them – looking at the people's physiques and states I didn't think they could do any harm. The people looked sick and not in the best shape. I wondered what happened here. Our land had survived many conflicts, but everything looked well-ordered. Aunt Noli used to say that it was this organization that started everything, this crazy pursuit of putting things in order, when things should be free. I think my aunt would like Elikya, especially the fashion and how they just didn't care.

There was nothing to see really, it was just sand and weak

houses everywhere and people looking at us like they were begging. He showed us the different houses of the leaders and explained how the community got together to build them. I wondered where they found the strength because they all looked pale, even though they came in different tones they all looked bloodless.

"This the reservoir ... we come here, and we grab some water to drink and to take a bath ... everyone is entitled to one bucket." He pointed at a small pond of water surrounded by cracked sand which was sucking the water almost dry. The water had sand particles in it. I could tell it by just looking at it that it wasn't very tasty or healthy. I always found it odd how leaders would talk about certain arrangements like they were benefiting the people, like it was some kind of generous act, when in reality it was just another humiliating gesture to keep the people obedient. I don't know why but it sounded familiar.

"Is this enough? For everyone?" Adowa asked while I was lost in my thoughts.

"So far, no complaints," Mahamba answered. He was looking at the same thing we were looking but with a different outlook. He looked at the leaders and everyone nodded.

"Are they allowed to complain?"

This was rubbing her the wrong way, and she couldn't pretend anymore.

"Of course, they can do anything they want to here." He opened his arms and stood by his statement.

Indeed, this looked like freedom, people were everywhere in the streets laughing and talking but what is there to do when you don't have much? I thought.

"Where are the churches? Hospitals? schools?" I could feel his body tense when I said 'schools'. I looked around and all I saw

46

was red sand and crippled houses. I didn't want to come across as someone who came from a modern and perfect land, since these things were still new to us too. I think my parents' generation was the first to attend school, before that their wisdom was only used to hate on the blackies.

"It's everywhere, look around ... We are the churches, the hospitals, the schools ... we learn from each other every day. We can find anything from within." He pointed at the people in the streets.

I remember that people from my land had to get accustomed to Mirror, he looked different from anything we had seen but here it was a mix of every tone we could ever imagine. I would be lying if I said they looked sad. They didn't look in the best shape, but they didn't look unhappy. Maybe this system worked.

"No churches?"

Adowa's eyelashes were fighting, she was perplexed. She didn't grow up in church, but the black side always told her to believe in something, and not having an institution to guide the people was strange to her.

"We believe in hope ... We wait for things."

He calmly answered us and scratched his beard. He was skinny like the others; you could tell even through his big cover-ups. He had a beard, but it was dispersed, hair everywhere, not organized. It seemed rough, like ingrown hair was growing and it was itching.

"We also believe in hope, but we make sure that when the things we pray for come that we know how to use them."

I was referring to books, but I could tell that he wasn't fond of the word 'praying'.

"'There is no better school in life than life itself.'" He quoted someone and then glanced at the people who were getting along and laughing.

It was rare to see that in Rhodesia but still I felt like Elikyans deserved more.

"I understand." I paused and nodded. This place didn't concern me. I had to go back to my aunt and child. "You said that you welcome people ... Who are these people? Where do they come from?"

"They come from every land – they are fleeing wars, persecution."

He smiled proud of offering a home to the people who needed one.

"Refugees?"

"No, we don't call them that." Cabinda intervened. His tall stature allowed him to have some kind of power that equated to Mahamba's influence.

"So, what do you call them?"

"By their names." It was the warmest thing Mahamba had said the whole day, I wondered if they memorized everyone's names in this land. It was already hard enough to memorize eighteen leaders and a Pastor Philips wannabe.

"I see. Thank you for everything you have done for us. Adowa is delighted by your offer to stay but we need to go back."

I was ready to head back to Harlow's house and share our goodbyes. I was speaking on her behalf, but I had to do it because I knew the rebels in us would find it alluring to stay and fight for this people.

"There is something that we would like your help with. Even though we are content with our system ... There is something we lack ... We are facing hardships ... Our people are dying," Cabinda confessed.

Mahamba looked at him, giving him a sign that he wasn't

48

supposed to be so candid.

"Of course –there are no hospitals," Adowa stated, rudely. She made the same gesture Mahamba had earlier when he had been trying to showcase Elikya as a perfect land.

"There is poverty." Cabinda ignored her and concluded his tirade. "Look around ... Poverty everywhere."

The scenario changed, even though Mahamba earlier spoke proudly of the peace and union between their people, they couldn't hide the penury.

"What's poverty?" Adowa asked.

It was starting all over again, that unawareness of what's happening around us. I think I knew the meaning. Growing up I had thought black people lived in penury, but I learned that the segregation didn't affect them so much financially, more like power wise.

"Privation ... deprivation ... impoverishment ... neediness."

He named different synonyms which revealed he had read something. There's no way they knew all these words and didn't read at all.

"See, we don't care about separation ... Power dynamics. This tribe has more ... This family has more. We are just leaders caring for our people. We have bigger problems here. We have people dying." He was being a bit condescending towards us and what we stood for but since our original set-up had failed no offense was taken.

"And how can we help?" Adowa humbly asked.

This was starting to feel like a trap.

"The people are hungry. We have been waiting for rain for years but nothing. But we have a feeling it will come soon, and we need your help. We know Rhodesians are handy and known for producing."

It was the first time they had complimented us on anything. Although, he was saying positive things, he wasn't smiling.

"Our population is sedentary. They are weak. They can't produce. Our soil is ready to cultivate."

He was leading us towards the farm areas. The plants seemed weak and lifeless. The unbearable warmth from the wind didn't allow us to think properly. I couldn't breathe. Everything was deadly dry. There was nothing greenish to decorate this area. The more we walked, the more I could see how barren the plain was, how hot the sand at our feet. It sifted through my footsteps like flour. It was a hopeless brown area. There was not even red sand to give the locals some kind of passion to fight against this dry spell.

"We don't have any seeds," Adowa stated.

"We have the seeds. We just need your stamina. We know about all your good deeds. How you are good in hands and everything you have done for your people."

Cabinda inspected Adowa from head to toe and congratulated her but not in an accommodating manner. Adowa was known everywhere, her story touched people from many lands, but in the black community, she was just the mad woman who braided every girl's hair.

"Listen Adowa, your leadership is impressive, I think we can count you for greater things. We want you, both of you, to help us cultivate and grow crops so we can live a sustainable life ... then you guys are free to go."

Benguela stepped in to make it seem it wasn't a threat, but it was too late. We could feel we were not completely free, and we had no choice.

"And what happens if we don't?"

Adowa could sense the same and directed her anger towards Mahamba.

"Adowa is out of shape, she has been through a lot in the past days, I also don't think I can do this. I spent most of my days in school. We need more people competent for this."

I touched Adowa's back to show that I had her back.

"There is someone who can help," Mahamba stated with a smirk.

"Someone?"

I had no idea who they were talking about. I noticed that the group got smaller while we were walking. Two leaders showed up again with someone I wasn't expecting but I couldn't say I wasn't happy to see a familiar face.

"Theo?"

I wanted to hug him, but I stopped myself because I didn't know what his presence meant here. I just hoped he had good news.

They handed Theo to us like he was a prisoner. We walked to Harlow's home in silence; maybe the mystical power was in the whole land. Everything was getting strange and weird. Theo seemed like he was holding some kind of information, and he was waiting for us to be in private. To be honest, Theo always seemed like he wanted to tell me something, and in the back of my mind, I still thought he loved me.

Harlow opened the door, not surprised to see Theo. She always seemed like she was a step ahead of us, like she already knew what was going to happen; she was just making sure we are on the right track.

The windows of her house were always closed as though people were afraid of each other. Wooden sticks were nailed

51

on top of the windows, just enough for people to not gossip. The lateral windows were between houses so there was little privacy. The main room was always dark, forcing us to speak very low, almost whispering.

"Theo what happened? What are you doing here?" Adowa snapped.

"Is Mirror okay?" I questioned him.

"They took Gunda ... Gunda is also here, he is in custody."

He took a long relaxing breath like he had been holding the information for days and hadn't had anyone he could trust. He didn't mention Mirror or anyone from home, which was alarming.

"Gunda?? What you mean? What is Gunda doing here?" Adowa continued to demand information.

"We came a few days ago, looking for you guys, we were worried. The moment we arrived the leaders of the land took Gunda, and I have been staying at their house." He sat down without even acknowledging Harlow.

"It happens. They arrange a place for guests to stay but it is a trap. While you are there, they pay attention to your every move," Harlow shared and helped us understand it. "So ... what did Gunda do? What was the crime?"

I was calmly and slowly processing everything.

"That story that we used to hear when we were kids, remember? About the white man that was killed by a black man ... it was Gunda ... years ago, he was still young ... he killed the man ... he confessed to me, on our way here."

Theo was only speaking to me only, for a few minutes he took me to back to our times, when we were just naïve white kids, before we joined this snowball of antagonism.

"Where exactly did you have this conversation?" Adowa

wondered. She aggressively placed her hands in the table.

"I don't know, there were trees everywhere. I guess at a forest ... We stopped to rest a bit."

"Caputo," Harlow confirmed.

"What's Caputo?" Theo asked.

"It's a mystical forest, it makes people tell the truth and confess their secrets. Some force influences you ... Gunda was under the influence," I explained.

Theo was silent; he was probably thinking about what he had confessed himself.

"Gunda didn't just kill a white man ... he was very young at the time and his dad had just passed away – he was sick – we then found out that his condition was caused by injections that white people were administrating."

Adowa and every black person knew about this, but they stood by Gunda. I wondered why if he wasn't kept in prison in our land why his crime was so important here?

"Back then everything was peaceful, but the whites noticed our sharpness, our mental capacity, and invited us to teach at their schools. But before we could enter the premises, we had to take some vaccinations that, according to them, it was meant to protect us from their environment, or any virus we might catch on their side. But it was genetically engineered to control our anger. They were so scared of us. We were so harmless. I still don't understand." Adowa paused. She was reliving everything.

"I really don't think they knew the outcome, but it caused some people to inherit a cell disorder which affected all major organs with a disease. Gunda's father was one of the first victims."

I had never heard Adowa being so impartial, I could see a lot of growth in her. It was the first time she acknowledged that white people might not have entirely bad intentions, they just wanted to protect their people, including me.

"Gunda killed the man who was behind the idea of creating those injections."

Theo didn't question Adowa's story. We all just sat listening to her carefully, she was the memory institute of the black side. At some point, she was having so many outbursts and tantrums that people stopped listening to her but when she came to her senses, just like now, it was liberating to hear her wisdom.

"No ... no ... he didn't kill the man that was behind the idea ... he killed the person he had access to ... someone with a family ... he killed the man who administered the injections ... a servant ... someone who was told what to do."

She shook her head. Adowa was fighting her own brain with this; I could tell that this thing took her back. She remained impartial but still held Gunda accountable.

"It's okay. We will talk to Gunda to understand everything. We will see what we can do but now we need to focus on what the leaders want."

Harlow sensed the tension and how hard was this for Adowa and tried to put us on back on track.

"They want us to grow crops, to help them," I gushed, but I had a feeling Harlow knew all about it.

"Yes. I know. I knew them capturing Adowa and then letting her free ... It was too easy ... I know these people ... They don't care what Adowa did ... They wanted something from you." She sounded like she had seen this before. I thought that growing up with Thriller made her this mature woman but now I think it was something else.

Theo was going to stay with us. I don't how I felt about him and me in the same house. I don't know how I felt about seeing him at all. Even though whenever I saw Theo, I felt peaceful, I had a feeling he was hiding something. With Vince, I was always worried – like he was some kind of omen.

It was almost dawn. I couldn't sleep. I didn't have the guts to ask Theo what really brough him here. I was sitting on the porch, and I sensed him approaching behind me.

"How is everyone? How is Caleb?"

I kept avoiding mentioning Mirror.

"He is fine, they grow up so fast, everyone is fine Jodi ... Don't worry"

"What brought you here? Your family needs you."

I inspected his eyes trying to understand him. What makes a grown man leave his family behind to go to another land? Love?

"I was the last person you saw before you left, so I had to make sure you were okay."

"You didn't have to, but I am glad you came."

"You don't need to be strong for me. I know you." He held me like I was this small thing and pulled me into his arms. I relaxed into his warmth.

"I need to ask you something ... what did you confess in Caputo? What was your secret?"

I pulled back from him and faced him. I was his Caputo now; he couldn't lie to me. He was influenced by our love.

"I said ... I ... I ... I am still in love with you."

I knew Theo still loved me, like I loved him but hearing that he was still 'in love' was different. I imagined how difficult it was for him all these years to watch me from afar live a completely different life. I rested my face on his chest, and I wanted to fall asleep there.

The next day, we sat down with Mahamba and agreed to start farming as soon possible, with one condition – that we were allowed to see Gunda.

They escorted us to the prison but only allowed me to go inside. Harlow warned me about them always being strategic and how they would move. They would change the rules, to whatever they pleased. I wasn't allowed to see Adowa when she was in prison, but I was allowed to see Gunda, which was confusing. The prison wasn't very different from the one Rhodesia. In the same way, it was below ground to literally send the message that whoever committed a crime was less than human.

It was crowed, dark and noisy. I had a strong feeling of *deja vu* as though I had lived through the situation before. I wasn't sure if it was an illusion or memory – the experience took me back to when I visited my dad and Vince. Both previous experiences had not been pleasant, and both had humiliated me, and tested my faith. It's a very weird feeling when someone tests the way you see life and try to make you join their anger and bitterness.

I started walking slowly; maybe this was a trap for me. Perhaps I had committed a crime; it all depended on people's perceptions. I saw all kinds of people in the cells: gypsies, refugees, hippies, and the likes. I wondered who told us to categorize people like that, how can you look at someone and automatically shred them into a name. As I was approaching his cell, I felt nervous about how he was going to treat me. I always felt like I owed something to Gunda. Maybe I should have saved my sister, I should have protected her, it was the least I could do.

"Jodi."

He called me but I felt like he wasn't certain of my name, I really think he thought it was Juvey. He wasn't sure if I was there or not. We both were looking at each other like we were wondering how she would age.

"Gunda, how are you? We are going to get you out of here."

I leaned towards his cell. I wasn't certain of my promise, but I had to give him some hope.

"It's okay, don't worry! How is Adowa? How are you? Did you manage to find the cure for Mirror?"

He touched my fingers through the bars.

"Everyone is okay ... Everything is fine ... Let's talk about you."

"I guess one day ... I had to pay for this."

He took a deep breath and seemed ready to share a lot that I didn't know.

"No ... you paid it, long ago ... In our land ... You were in prison ... I remember hearing about it."

My eyes started dancing trying to understand. I was always afraid to learn something new.

"Yes ... I was ... but I didn't serve my sentence ... Juvey ... Juvey helped me get out." When he said 'Juvey', he stopped touching my hand.

"Juvey."

What about her? I didn't want to learn anything bad about my sister. I was at peace with whatever happened. I forgave my father and myself, but I knew it was up to Gunda and Juvey to also do the same, I couldn't impose that on them.

Gunda seemed different, just like Adowa he didn't have the same anger towards white people. Something about this place was changing them. He sat on the dusty floor and made a sign for me to do the same. Our backs were so close, and his mouth was literally one inch from my ear so I could hear him whisper loudly:

"I saw red, just like the red of the sand of Elikya. It was as though I was engulfed in a big red bubble of hatred and grief. He

57

was standing at the tunnel, packing up the injection kits into boxes. It was the end of the day, and he was ready to go. I wish I had arrived a few minutes later so that he would have survived my anger. I wasn't a killer – I had never killed anyone. I was just in pain. I loved my dad – my dad was everything to me. I just felt like I had to do something, to show how much I cared for my dad.

The man was older than me, but my height allowed me to have some kind advantage over him and I used it. I had heard so many times that we, the blacks, were so strong. In that moment, I believed it. I felt powerful – like I could do something.

He turned his back to me as he packed the materials. I got closer to him. I wish he had sensed me approaching, but he didn't. I was so angry; I could hardly see him. All I could see were the syringes still scattered on the table, and I grabbed them.

I stabbed him in the back twelve times. I could almost feel the blood stop moving through his veins. Even though his back was muscular and stiff, my anger allowed me to puncture his skin.

He turned to face me, and his confused eyes met my angry ones. He had no idea what he had done to deserve it. I could see all the veins in his body – white people are transparent. Even though I pretended for years that I had been right, and even though my people backed me up, I knew, right after I stabbed him, that he didn't deserve it.

I felt the two white men grabbing me from behind and pulling me away from the man. In that moment I was glad that they grabbed me because I couldn't feel my legs anymore – it was like I had transferred all my energy of my body into my upper body – my hands and arms. The white men took me to prison. I think I was the first black person they got. I felt like they enjoyed it – they didn't even care for the man.

The prison was empty. There was a breeze that I felt whenever someone came to visit me, and a distant door swung open. Otherwise, I was in that stuffy atmosphere all day and night. All the blacks were talking about taking me out of there, but I didn't really care. My dad was gone and there was nothing worth living for. Until I met your sister...

One day, a petite, white girl entered the premises. I heard her slippers that clattered against the floor. Then I watched her going to every cell, kindly offering the few inmates bowls of soup. The food smelled good – I can still remember that smell.

She finally arrived at my cell and offered me a bowl. As she approached, I began to memorize her face. She had a long chin, the kind that makes you want to hold it and kiss her. Her skin was glowing. It was a cream ivory that turned to almond in the shaft of sunlight falling in from the skylight. Her mouth was wide, but her lips were small, contoured with carnation red.

I declined the soup by shaking my head. I couldn't trust them. She didn't seem offended, somehow, I feel like she understood me. She just smiled and left the bowl on the floor. That smile lit her face and confirmed her beauty. I wasn't ready to admit that I found a white girl beautiful. I couldn't think about it. Maybe the days in the cell had made me aroused by things I used to despise.

I ended up having the soup. It was hot and full of veggies with no meat at all. I wanted to taste some meat, but the soup still filled me up.

After that, I kept thinking about her. She was curvy for a white girl. They had access to all kinds of food, but generally, they were still slim. But she was different. She always wore a long skirt. Later I learned that she hid certain things under the skirt that the inmates asked her for.

Every week, I would wait for that smell of soup and to see her face. I kept thinking of ways to decline the soup more gently or to thank her.

One day she arrived and tried to tempt me with the food.

"Here ... Have some ... Don't be proud ... It's just soup ... I can try some if you want." She tasted it to show me that the soup was harmless. She wasn't scared of me.

"I know. I've had it before." I placed my arms between the grids to receive the soup. She stayed until I finished to collect the bowl.

"Next time, I will bring something stronger ... you need meat ... you are getting weak," she murmured, making sure the guards didn't hear her.

Who was this girl? And how could she talk to me like that? I memorized the days and times she came. Usually, the sun was still bright when I heard her footsteps. What stuck in my mind was the fact that she knew I had considered the food to be poison and she hadn't been offended at all. Seeing her was the best part of my day.

I didn't want to admit it, but I was attracted to a white girl. My obsession went from the smell of hot soup to the faint scent of her hair, which smelled like homemade cake.

"Here. Hide it well!" One day, she appeared, suddenly, and handed me food that smelled like meat.

"What are you doing here today?"

"I came to give you this." She spoke as though getting dried meat for me was no big deal, even though she risked her life. It wasn't a safe place for anyone, especially a woman, a white woman.

That day, as I ate, we sat down together, with our backs turned towards the cell bars.

"Don't you want to know what I did to be here?" I probed her. I wanted to understand this girl.

"Don't you wonder what I did to be here?" she replied. She was right, bringing soup to prisoners wasn't a task you would delegate to a well-behaved citizen. Later, I learned that she had got in trouble in school for asking about black people's access to education and the prison rounds were her punishment.

"We all wonder … What makes a white girl come here three times a week to feed us. What have you done 'soup girl'?" I smiled. It was the first time I had smiled since my dad had passed. Then I panicked, realizing that I had disclosed my obsession with her by mentioning the exact number of times a week she had been coming. There was a brief silence before she spoke again.

"Soup girl'? Is that what you guys call me?" She laughed very hard, and I could spot, even with her back to the bars, that she was clutching her belly.

"Well … That's what I call you. Thanks for the beef."

"I won't lie, this was a punishment but now I kinda enjoy it. I get to have another perspective on life. I get to help people who lost all their hope."

" Hope." I repeated, and it took me back to my last memories with my dad.

"Yes, hope … I believe in hope … we need to believe in something," she whispered. I had never met anyone so pure in my life.

"By the way I don't come three times a week, I come only twice … But I can try to come more." She realized I had been paying attention. I don't think she cared about me being black as much as I cared about her being white. She just didn't care about anything.

"Do you believe someone can kill someone and be a good person?"I didn't dare to look her in eyes. I was afraid I had scared her.

"Hmmm ... if you asked me years ago, I would have said no." She took a long breath and tried to be as honest she could. "But now ... I don't think so ... people are moved by feelings ... it can be auto-defense ... grief ... anger." I could tell she had spent time talking to other inmates. "But only you know who you are ... Some people won't ever accept that you are a good person because doing that would make them accept that they had been wrong, and their harsh judgement and assumption had been uncalled for." Her voice was calm, while explaining. I had never listened anyone with so much attention and obedience. I wondered how old she was and marveled at her maturity.

"What's your name?"

There had been nothing else to say. I had just wanted to give a name to the woman I fell in love with.

"Juvey ... Juvey Collins," she had said, proudly, and she knew what her name meant. She was Lawyer Collin's daughter. I couldn't lie, I was scared of her, not because who her father was but because of how wise and pure she was; that combination was deadly. Pure and innocent people scare most people because you can't believe that people like this exist. You can't fathom that people live in this land and still choose to not be affected by it.

"What's your name?"

"Gunda." I was never given a surname.

"Gunda ... Whatever you did ... It's all part of a cycle ... You unconsciously or consciously do something to someone, they get hurt and retaliate, now you are hurt ... They forgive us, but we are not ready to forgive them, and it becomes a cycle of hurting

62

people. Forgive yourself."

She had basically summarized what happened in her own words without even having the details. I didn't need a trial – my sentence was falling in love with a white woman.

I could feel her head shifting against the bars, and her scalp touched my head. Her hair was thin, empty, and lightweight – like nothing. It wasn't like the hair of the girls I was used to. I could grab a black girls' hair and my fingers would be fighting the threadlike strands growing from her scalp.

After that day, things changed. Sometimes she didn't have a reason to come, she would just come. We would spend hours talking. One day, she offered a meal to the guard, in exchange for entering my cell to braid my hair. I didn't know she could do black people's hair. It hurt my scalp at first, but her fingers running around my fur made me relax and forget what I did. I wasn't a killer or a black man when I was with her. Sometimes I wondered if she had some kind of fetish and if she just wanted to be with a black man but, later, seeing what she was willing to do for me, I released my insecurities.

I didn't mind being in prison anymore, if I saw her. If I left and went to the dark side, I wouldn't see her often. My heart would beat fast whenever I heard her long skirt drag all the dust in the floor, it would make a weird sound, like she was fighting the air with her legs.

I could still taste dried meat stuck between my teeth, I imagined the meat in her groin area and how it would benefit from her own body spices. I couldn't stop thinking about her. It wasn't just lust. When you lust after a woman and you have the chance to experience her wisdom, you instinctively turn to her. You desire her, you yearn for her, you crave her.

63

Gunda paused his tale.

"What happened? Tell me." I needed to hear more. I enjoyed getting to know my sister from his perspective. I missed her. I had no idea what was going on my sister's life. Maybe I hadn't cared. I had been so obsessed with my own life – getting married to Theo – that nothing really fazed me. I can't remember when she changed but I remember her long skirts. I had made fun of them, when I had no idea she was wearing them for a noble cause.

Gunda spoke once more.

"As time passed, she started to ask more questions about my case and wanted to help and she did."

When he said, 'she did,' it sounded like a death sentence.

"So, she talked to my dad and my dad talked to Pastor Philips?" I was already creating the picture.

"Yes. She convinced Pastor Phillips to let me go. I was only eighteen. Your sister was very smart. I think she could do anything she wanted. I don't understand why she wanted to waste her time helping me." When you are in a critical situation, its customary to put your own self down.

"She convinced Pastor Philips that it would make him look good – you know whites and their egos – and be seen as holy and forgiving."

He sounded like Adowa. I think by now I have become a mixed woman, because they didn't see me as white anymore.

"I know." I bowed my head.

"Bad people mimic good people. They play the victim, and they use your misfortune in their favor. They rely on the coincidences that favor them." He was quoting Juvey. It sounded like something she would say.

"And they will never change."

64

"There's something I want you to know. After I was dis-charged, your father found out about our relationship and asked her to stop seeing me, otherwise I would be sent back to prison. First, she disappeared, but with time, we started to see each other again."

He stopped; he realized that the next chapter about this story was going to be about my dad killing my sister. I reflected that we should be the ones feeling less than other people. Juvey wasn't better than Gunda because she came from a white family; not at all, she was a woman who was killed by her own father.

"It's okay, Gunda ... Just rest. We will try to come as much as we can."

I noticed how telling this story was affecting him. I touched his shoulder trying to calm him down. I imagined that me being there reminded him of Juvey's visits. I didn't want to hear anymore right now.

I wasn't sure if Gunda had known that Juvey had been preg-nant. It didn't matter anymore. There are things we will never know, and we just need to accept that. Sometimes I think my dad asked Juvey to terminate her pregnancy, she refused, and he killed her. Sometimes I think my dad just killed her without even knowing she was pregnant. Whatever it was, the soup girl, the shampoo girl, was dead.

Chapter 4

They brought the three of us to the same area they had showed us a few days earlier. We were treated like prisoners and our sentence was to grow something in this dead land. The ground was so cracked it reminded me of peeling the skin from my dad's feet when I was toddler, when everything was fine.

The weather was so hot it made everything was unbearable. But we would see the occasional plant somewhere, but very small, which gave us hope. It wasn't the kind of weather that would make you sweat, though; it was dry. The worst thing was trying to breathe; I felt my heart and chest about to burst in the dry heat. I leaned on Theo's arm; I was about to faint.

"First, you plough the field," Mahamba ordered and pointed at the extensive, parched field in front of us. He handed us different iron tools to help us start. I held one of them and it felt very heavy; I wasn't built for this.

"Cunene, Huila and Namibe will stay with you to help in anything you need."

He turned and left.

Why were those three chosen? Were they the most fit? I was

alert.

"Let's start! We have a lot of work to do."

Cunene tried to motivate us. He was tall and well built. He had robust eyelids and a scar on his right eye. I guessed that he would eventually share the story of that scar.

We dropped down to the lifeless ground with our old-fashioned tools and started turning the soil.

The work was dirty. Soil got under. My fingernails, and my clothes, which I had been exhausting myself by washing every single day, were filthy. There was no way to be clean doing this task. I just hoped that their true intentions were pure and clean.

I could feel different types of insects crawling on my body, and even when they left, I could still sense more coming. It gave me constant chills. I also spotted skeletons of different animals everywhere, and I wondered about them.

"What happened to all these animals?"

I just couldn't keep my mouth shut. We spent hours working in silence, looking at each other, so I had the need to make conversation.

Cunene explained to us, continuing his ploughing: he seemed to really want this to work.

"Well, the drought affects everything around us. Especially this one because it has been going on for years. There has been no water. The water is not even enough for us – imagine how it is for the animals. There is also no food and without food the plants and animals can't survive."

"And the few who survive. What are you planning to do with them?" I asked.

The sweat dripped into my eyes from my hair, and I tried to clean it with my dirty hands. I ended up irritating my eyes with soil. Adowa came to help by blowing, but I felt my eyes turning red. Theo was just watching; he didn't want to show the leaders that we were close, to protect me, I guess.

"Just keep them alive. Feed them. That's why we are doing this. They are kept in town with us to survive. Here, in these conditions, they would eventually die. If the animals survive, they will reproduce and help reestablish things." He explained this with the same patience that he was investing in loosening and turning the soil.

"What happened before? How did the situation get to this point?"

"I guess we got comfortable. We thought we would have certain things forever. We didn't take care of them. We had no idea that the drought would last so many years." He scratched his scar. I could tell he had been reading. I looked at him suspiciously; they were not telling the truth about the books.

Namibe spoke. "We took it for granted. It feels like the land is punishing us for how we treated it. Our Elikya lost hope."

Namibe was probably Cunene's age, but he seemed more reserved.

"What if the rain never comes? People are dying. They should eat the few animals that are still available before something happens."

Theo wasn't very emotional and didn't care about things like hope or faith, he resorted to logic.

"We can't eat them ... we would never eat them ... We don't eat animals ... We eat what they produce ... They are our treasure ... Our property ... You wouldn't understand." Cunene started touching the soil aggressively.

"We understand, but people are dying," Adowa begged. She seemed to enjoy being busy with her hands, instead of her mind.

Being in prison must have been tedious.

"Animals are our family. Each family still has one animal. And we will make sure that they still own something," Cunene stammered.

It was hard for me to understand because if they saw them as family, how could they own them? Vince used to tell me about that when we had tutoring classes, but he said that segregation became their major focus; they didn't want to lose time with tradition beliefs that were stalling them.

"My family owns a cow. It's my dowry," Huila murmured and ended the conversation. Her curves gave her some kind of balance to sift cereal grains.

It was the first time I had heard how they categorized or named animals, and it showed a lot about their mindset. I wouldn't be surprised if they had names for each animal.

Harlow later explained that a dowry is a payment, such as property or animal, paid by the bride's family to the groom or his family at the time of marriage. Huila seemed too old to still be waiting to get married. It made me realize that I had never got married. With time, I had completely forgotten my dreams, and who I was.

We took a break, and they escorted us to another area where there was a big tree; bigger than anything I had seen. I always thought the black side was magical, but Elikya was full of surprises, how had this tree survived all the loss from the persistent dryness? It looked like many trees growing as one and its robust branches looked as though they could hold anyone. The tree was a monster, its leaves were unaffected by the weather and the circumstances, like the tree had his own character. They

69

told us to climb it, and this felt like another task.

"This is the sacred tree." Cunene introduced us to the old tree. You could tell it was old and it witnessed every change in the weather and in this land.

"Embondeiro," Huila said in their own dialect. The whole time they would talk in their language, probably about us.

"Come." Namibe gave me his hand to help me climb.

Theo seemed jealous, men were men in every situation, you could be fighting for your life, but they would still have trivial feelings. I placed my right hand on the lowest branch, and he pulled my body up, my legs on the hard walls of the tree and took another swing so that my whole body could fit into the trunk. I finally relaxed with my back against the tree, and I watched Theo struggle to come up. He was too manly to ask anyone for help.

The others continued to speak in their tongue. I tried to understand it, but I couldn't. Neither could Adowa, and especially not Theo.

We all managed to climb and when we settled into the branches, we enjoyed the breeze from the height of the tree. An ovary with an endocarp fell on the ground before I was able to catch it.

"What is that?" Adowa was curious. It seemed familiar, it probably reminded her of similar fruits that she used to refine and use on her hair.

"It's a fruit ... The sacred fruit," Cunene shouted.

"Can I try it?" Adowa asked.

We had been told to avoid talking about food, but we were hungry. And I missed fruits, the moisture would be refreshing in this hopeless weather.

Cunene went down to grab it and gave it to Adowa. The skin

of the fruit had a hairy top layer, like animal fur.

"Can we grow more trees like this one? It's so strong! It can help with many things," Theo asked.

"No, there's only one. We can't grow anything like this ever again ... We tried ... Many times," Cunene said, while balancing his feet on the branch.

"We can learn new ways if we read about them," Theo insisted.

I was afraid they would get mad and not help us get down from the tree.

"You know how Mahamba feels about reading."

He mentioned Mahamba, emphasizing that this was one man's decision.

"I know but what about you, Cunene? How do you feel about it?"

Theo held one arm tight in one branch, afraid that the tension of the conversation would cause him to fall.

"I don't know. I just want my people to be safe, to be well-fed and to improve their nutrition."

"Books are problematic. We don't want problems. We just want peace." Huila helped Cunene, speaking softly.

Cunene continued to speak. "I wasn't always like this ... I remember learning to read and then one day my mom stopped teaching me. Growing up I learned that it became a competition of who knows more 'I have read 50 books', 'I have read 100 books'. People started asking for acknowledgements and recognition. They started asking for titles. It was disturbing our peace." Cunene seemed embarrassed by not being able to read.

"It's not the books ... it's the people," Adowa clarified, while touching the sacred fruit.

"I know but Mahamba does his best in trying to keep our land in peace. To keep people controlled ... in a good way." He seemed

to respect Mahamba's ideology, but he was not fully down with
it.

Namibe broke in then. "Reading does not fuel egos ... reading
is humility and willingness to learn."

In Namibe, we had a potential ally. He wasn't afraid of his
beliefs. I looked over to Theo and Adowa to check if they heard
him.

"We don't want problems. We just want to understand."
Adowa tried to be a peacemaker, for once.

"At least the Book ... The Book is the start ... You want the rain
... You talk about hope and faith, but you don't believe in the
Book?"

Theo echoed Adowa's soft and understanding voice and
pleaded. Sometimes I forgot the 'good boy' in Theo; the church
boy I once fell in love with.

"The Book was ... was intense you know ... it created different
ways of expressing ... I remember people going door to door to
explain the Book ... they would force people into their thinking
... then there were different churches ... a competition of whoever
understood the Book better ... so we abolished everything that
drove us to competition." Namibe was definitely quoting
Mahamba but as much he wanted to come across as a faithful
servant to the main leader, he wasn't fooling us.

"So there where churches before?" I started probing him.

"Yes. I remember going to one."

Cunene was young; therefore he could give us a perspective
on when everything changed.

The wise Namibe saved Cunene by changing the topic.

"It has been a long day. We should finish up, then rest and
come back tomorrow."

A few days later, they finally gave us the seeds, and we started planting on the ground, literally. There were still a few plants and we tried to save them by cutting specific parts – the roots – in the hope that they would grow. Everything was about hope. It was a tiring job, way more exhausting than fighting for black people's rights.

I thought about our situation. The ground was powdery, and the air was dry and blew heat into my face. I was red and I wasn't coping well but I had no choice. This wasn't a job for only six people. Where were the other leaders? Why were those three were chosen to be here and the others weren't? I was intrigued by the whole system of leaders and learning about them helped the hours pass faster in that dry area. Cunene shared that every leader had a story and for some convenient reason Mahamba was the hero in those stories. Cunene said that when he was young, an animal had bitten him near his eyes and Mahamba had ordered his servants to find plants to heal Cunene's wound. He said that the wound was so deep that it had almost affected his sight. I wondered how Mahamba had saved eighteen people ... eighteen favors or eighteens debts?

"It's raining ... it's raining," Adowa shouted repeatedly.

We all look at the clean and simple sky and saw nothing. I opened my mouth and tried to taste it, but nothing was coming.

"Where?"

Cunene stopped planting, looked around and opened his arms.

"Don't mind her." I calmed him down. "Adowa, what's got into you?"

I was afraid she was having one of her relapses, she had been doing so well.

"It's a declaration ... I declare that I am enough. I have enough. I am in the right place, at the right time, doing the right thing. I

73

can do hard things. I allow myself to be more fully me.

I believe in myself. I am grateful for another day of life. I am worthy of what I desire.

I choose myself." She was citing someone, I wasn't sure who, but she seemed light, and her words were calming.

"You're in a good mood today."

Theo smiled and headed to the sacred tree, he was intrigued by it, like it was his new vehicle

"It's raining ... I can feel it."

Adowa smiled and lay on the ground, contemplating the sky.

"Explain what you mean? Do you see anything?"

Cunene continued to look at the sky and nothing was there.

"If we want something to happen ... we need to believe it's already happening." Adowa teased us and we tried to join her madness. I knew she had high intuition, but I wasn't sure what she was doing.

"Where did you learn that?"

I got close to her and tried to understand.

"In prison ... Kofi taught me that."

She continued to smile, like she was a high on something. I never asked her who Kofi was, but she would mention him from time to time. I knew he was a product of her imagination because if he had really existed how come she never went to see him? She was aware of her delusional tendencies, and it wasn't the first time she had an imaginary friend; I had met many through the years – Raúl, Nilson, Bubas ... those are the names I can remember.

"JEZU NGO, MUENE UA TUITIA ... U TUENDESA UM MUENHU IÚ ... KANA-KU DINGI DIKAMBA DIENGI ... INGANA JEZU, MUENE KAMBA DIETU ... JEZU NGÓ, JEZU NGÓ ... LATUSAKE MIXIMA IETU ... JEZU NGÓ, JEZU NGO."

She started singing which meant she wanted to be left alone. She had been clear-headed for many days, and that wasn't like her.

I left them trying to understand Adowa, which we had all struggled to do for many years. I joined Theo at the sacred tree. Behind me, I could hear Adowa say 'Jezu'. Aunt Noli told me that it in the beginning it was only about 'Jezu' and then the Book told us about so many holy men than we starting referring to them as 'they'.

I offered my arms for Theo to hold them and pull me towards his branch. I held his body like it was a branch. He still smelled the same. Adowa used to tell me that being intimate with someone consolidated the connection, however, we had never been physical. But I had never felt so strongly about a man. Even when I was still with Vince, I would feel a certain way towards Theo. I always wondered if it would a go away, and if Theo could sense it, or if Vince cared. I had made sure Theo never noticed that he still had an impact me. I was committed to Vince, and I had a child. I wasn't a girl anymore.

"How is Mariane doing?"

I was just trying to make conversation, to not make the situation more awkward than it was. I thought about the day that Theo came to my house to tell me he was going to be with another girl.

He took a long breath before answering. "She is okay."

"She must be worried. Did you tell her where you were going?" I avoided eye contact because I was embarrassed of putting him in that situation. He didn't answer me and just chose to look at every part of my face. I had not seen myself in a mirror for years. I had stopped caring about my looks long ago. Vince had never cared for my looks, but Theo made me feel beautiful by just looking at me, even after almost twenty years.

"How do you think this tree survived? It doesn't make sense."

He looked for other things to fixate his eyes on and started analyzing the branches.

"They said it's the sacred tree."

If Theo lived on the black side he would stop asking questions and just accept nature as it is.

"Some leaves are burned. I think there was a fire here. Maybe they tried to demolish it." This was definitely Theo's new car.

Namibe appeared and started speaking. "We told you ... It's the drought ... It affects everything. We are living the longest drought. It can dry even the strongest, largest, and most sacred tree. The weather makes it flammable."

Namibe was admiring the tree and touching its grotesque skin. We weren't familiar with drought. This had been the first time we left Rhodesia. We only knew white and black weather, and both were slightly pleasant.

"Namibe ... how do you survive? Do you have another source of food? If this doesn't work, or even if it does, it might take months. We don't want you to get your hopes high." Theo looked down to face Namibe.

"Mahamba does a distribution of food every now and then, but his stock is running out ... so we need to be prepared," Namibe revealed.

"So, Mahamba has access to food and he chooses when to give to you guys?"

I didn't know Theo was so brave. I spotted Cunene looking at us and getting ready to join us.

"He makes sure we are fed," Namibe emphasized.

"And he makes sure you obey him," Theo declared, before I could stop him.

I made a sign for him to get down from the tree because Cunene was coming, and we had finished for the day.

At home, Harlow prepared some juice from the sacred tree. It made my teeth shiver; it was heavy, and it had a lot of pulp. She said it helped with their hunger and it made people feel full for a long time.

Benguela came over with some books about injections that other lands were experimenting with, so we could study more for Gunda's case. I still wasn't sure what we could do if there were no lawyers nor witnesses but I trusted Harlow's gut.

"I found something about Demetrius here," Theo pointed out while holding a book.

I wondered where all these books came from. If they had a food stock, they probably also had a book stock.

"What does it say?"

Adowa was curious because the disease was prevalent on the black side.

"Apparently there were vaccinations created to fight the disease and later, those injections contained some kind ... of ... I don't know ... a virus maybe ... and started spreading a virus that in one way or another and made people's cells sick."

Theo tried to explain but he was very careful with his words because the whites had been accused of spreading Demetrius.

I responded. "So, the injections weren't to make people immune to the virus but to protect them from Demetrius? It makes sense because if we were once accused of polluting the ocean to cause the rise of red flies, and cause Demetrius ... I think we would ensure that no one on our side would get Demetrius?" I tried to explain myself clearly.

Harlow was completely lost so she kept reading.

"But ... we were also told that the injections were to control our anger? So, which one is it?" Adowa probed us like we had an answer for her.

"Here ... it also says that people with Demetrius are immune ... protected from 'Umntwana uyagula'," read aloud.

"Is that what it is called?"

Harlow looked like she heard that name before.

"Yes ... look ... we need to focus ... how can all this help Gunda? Are we trying to say that he had the right to kill a man because the man was responsible for spreading the disease ... when we all know, and Gunda even admits, that he knew he wasn't the one to blame for this ... and where are we going to explain all those things? Are we allowed to talk during his session?"

Theo had his fingers on his moustache trying to process everything.

"It's called Babemba ... listen ... you need to trust me ... we are allowed to stand up for someone in Babemba ... people just don't do it because they are afraid." Harlow reinforced her idea.

"Afraid of what?" I trusted her but I had to understand.

"Of not having access to certain things ... not receiving food ... if Mahamba feels like you somehow tried to challenge him ... you will suffer the consequences."

I realized as she spoke that she was talking about herself; she was a victim of his.

We were disgusted by what we heard, and we swallowed it just to avoid knowing more about this faulty system.

" 'The oppressors, pretending to be generous, need injustice to continue, so that their 'generosity' continues.'"

Theo switched books and read a quote written by an influential leader of a land called Kunami.

"Here ... it also says that it's possible that some people were born with a random small mutation in one of their genes which causes 'Umntwana uyagula'."

Adowa tried to lighten the mood. Was it possible that Gunda's father and grandfather were born like this? We had all witnessed how nature sometimes doesn't have explanations. And we were not ready to admit that we were wrong about both sides, black and white. We stopped; the discussion was raising tensions. We had to sleep early to get ready for another long day.

I couldn't stop coughing. Cunene had told me that there were many diseases that being exposed to this area could cause. I wasn't sure if it was an allergy, but everything was making me sick – the injustice, the oppression, the dust, and the smell of dead animals in the air. Sometimes, I could feel the animals' hair suspended in the air.

I needed water to fight whatever virus or bacteria was trying to install itself in my body. Mahamba would send Moxico time from time to bring us water. At first I didn't want to drink their polluted water, but the heat was oppressive, and we had no choice. Moxico would struggle to carry the bowls of water, her small structure didn't allow to carry more, but seeing her coming from afar was one of the best parts of the day, apart from spending time in the sacred tree.

"You guys are almost done!" Moxico stated, while inspecting the whole area chosen for this upcoming miracle.

"Now we wait," Cunene said, while touching his sore back.

"It's been weeks, and nothing..." Theo complained.

"It takes months to grow things," Cunene continued, hope-fully.

I wondered how long our sentence was going to last.

"There is a season to grow," Namibe added.

They pronounced a lot of words incorrectly, which showed their lack of reading, but at the same time their wisdom showed otherwise.

"When will it be done? We can't be here forever."

Theo was getting impatient. He had a wife and son to go back to. And we were not sure what we were supposed to gain from this work. It had been implied that it was Gunda's freedom, but they never really confirmed this.

"You need to have hope ... Long ago there were two leaders ... *Chronos and Kairos* ... And they taught us that there is time that can be measured and there is time judged not by its duration, but by its importance and value. We are doing something noble here ... We appreciate everything you have done for us ... The moment is coming ... We can feel it ... The season of growth is coming."

Cunene looked over to Adowa, thanking her for affirmations, and her devotion to the work. We were all a bit tired of talking about hope and things we couldn't touch.

I continued to cough; Theo decided to accompany me back to the house.

"You need to rest."

He carefully placed me in the bed.

"I keep having this feeling that you have something to tell me ... is it about Mirror? I have avoided asking about him because I am afraid you have bad news."

I held his shirt and tried to stop coughing long enough to be able to say what I wanted to say. I thought about Mirror every

80

single day but the thought of something happening to him made me fearful of asking.

"No, Jodi. Mirror is fine! Trust me."

He held me like he was trying to hug me and at the same time show the sincerity in his words.

"So, what is it? Tell me." I begged him.

He paused for a few minutes.

"When I was staying at the leader's house, I passed by a room ... It was full of books. I think they are lying to us ... You can tell that Cunene and Namibe do read. Sometimes they make a few mistakes here and there, but they are smart ... They are being stimulated by something or someone. Think about it ... Where does Benguela gets all these books? Where? We are thankful but we should ask questions. And Harlow, can we really trust her?"

He withdrew from the hug and held my arms trying to wake me up from being too naïve.

"Yes ... They are reading – it's very telling. But I think we can trust Harlow ... She has been nothing but kind ... She allowed us to stay here with her." My gut told me to trust her but maybe I was influenced because she reminded me of Mirror.

"I think they might be using us for something ... They want something."

There is something about men being suspicious, it's like a protection shield, that they want you want to be safe and you just let them take control.

"Like what?"

"Dark plants."

He looked at the door, making sure no one was listening.

"I didn't bring any."

"But Gunda did."

He joined me under the fly nets.

"Where is it? Do you have it?"

"Yes," he said it in a way that I shouldn't ask any more questions or he couldn't reveal where he hid it.

He tucked me into bed and left.

The next morning, I asked Harlow to go fetch some water from the reservoir. I wanted to be alone with her so I could ask more questions. I didn't want to drink the water, but my cough was getting worse. I don't remember drinking the water direct from the sea, I remember seeing them using plants to treat water but here all the plants were dead. I looked around at other people drinking the poisonous and dirty water like they were so grateful for it. Vince used to tell me about leaders who would starve their people and make them so weak that their only escape was being a good servant. I placed my hands in the water, and I saw my reflection. I had aged. I wasn't blessed with black people's genes. You could tell that I was entering my forties. Me and Vince are the same age now. Dead people don't age.

"What are you thinking about?" Harlow noticed I was lost in my thoughts.

"So many things ... I don't even know where to start."

"How is the farming going?" she asked.

Harlow wasn't allowed to go. I wondered what Harlow did while we were out.

"It's a lot ... I am glad it is almost over." I abruptly changed the conversation. "Harlow, where does Benguela get all these books? I am very grateful for her help ... but..."

"The leaders have access to books. They have a library in their house."

She didn't hesitate; she would give me all the information to equip me the necessary tools for the so waited 'coup d'etat'.

"So, every leader can read them? But the people can't."

I felt like splashing the water all over.

"No. Mahamba reads to them!"

She wasn't as angry as I felt. Perhaps she had learned to accept the situation. I tried to process what she had said, and I wasn't sure how I felt about it. I knew that most leaders had controversial characters, but Mahamba surpassed all my expectations. He truly belittled people.

"I don't understand." I did but I wanted to be sure. I finally drank the water to swallow everything I just heard.

"They organize gatherings, and he reads different books to them. They are dependent on him," she said, with disgust.

I took a minute to process everything. There are acts so cruel that you wonder how someone could come up with them. My mind took me back to Book studies, where Pastor Philips would tell us his own perception of the verses, and I would always challenge him.

"And why do they accept that? Why they are okay with that? Before Mahamba became the main leader, there were people who would read, right? Cunene told me his mom taught him how to read and then she stopped ... I am pretty sure a lot of people still had the chance to learn."

I always assume that everyone is a rebel like me, willing to stand against the system. I remember Harlow reading at the house, so I was trying to find out how she learned.

"This is bigger than him. Other leaders before him started this a long time ago on the 27th of May the former leaders decided to kill everyone who knew more than them. First, they started with women, they said that they were not allowed to learn how to read. With time, they started to envy their own kind: men against men. Mahamba claims that they did this for our own good, so we wouldn't kill each other out of jealousy, so we wouldn't envy each other." She spoke calmly.

"Women were not allowed to read."

I paused for a few seconds; it was too much to digest.

"There is so much more ... We used to farm, we used to take care of our land ... One day Mahamba ordered that the leaders would be in charge of producing and delivering the harvest to our door. At first, it sounded like heaven ... We would be at home and food would come to us ... There would be no hard work ... We got comfortable, I guess."

While she explained, I remember seeing how the Elikyans enjoyed their free time. They spent most of their time drinking, playing cards, and talking, while becoming slower and slower.

"I see ... I am pretty sure he did that to win you over to offer his kindness, goodwill, service. A favor but at the same time expecting a favor in return."

I had seen this before.

"He wanted to control everything ... The quantity of the food for each house. He would starve us ... When people are hungry they don't think, they act on desperation ... We couldn't fight back."

"Harlow ... do you owe him any favors?"

I was scared of offending her. I looked into her eyes very quickly and then I looked away, embarrassed.

"I don't. And that's the issue! That's why he rules me out completely." She didn't seem to care. "I was very young when I arrived here. I came from a land where we were mostly black ... no whites, no colored, no mixed ... just black. But there is always something that makes us different ... and it shouldn't be honored, glorified, nor worshipped. We started celebrating

84

people with lighter complexions – they became our leaders. It got worse, we started applauding perfection, we were so vain and so into our looks that it went too far. When I was born, my parents didn't know what to do with me, when they noticed my patches … the more I lost pigment, the more they were worried about how our land was going to react. They had no choice. So they brought me to Elikya. They left me here." A tear fell from her right eye. She tried to hide it, but I noticed it.

"They were just trying to protect you."

I would do the same for my child. I nodded slowly, trying to show her that I understood her pain and also her parents' decision.

"I know. I have forgiven them long ago." She let more tears come but this time she didn't hide them. "Mahamba took me to his house and raised me … he became my mentor … he taught me how to read, how to speak and how to think like him. Years went by and he wanted to help me … take me to this healer Ngunza from another land … he was powerful and could try to remove my patches, but I refused. I used to read stories about other people with *thriller* and how society excluded them. Some were accused of wanting to be white. Some tried to change their skin and it gave them health complications. I didn't want to do anything about it. I just wanted to love myself."

"You did the right thing."

I thought about Mirror.

"Mahamba even invited me to be part of the leadership if I agreed to seek healing in the town of Nkamba. I said no, I liked my patches, I got used to them … they became me. This infuriated him … he wanted to be there for me, but I don't know, I just felt like it wasn't genuine … he wanted me to be indebted … So, he disowned me … he called me ungrateful."

She bowed her head like she was fighting her thoughts trying to understand if she did the right thing.

"You are not ungrateful."

"I never really cared for leadership. People have a problem when you have a different view, and you stand on your own ... They somehow think you are better than them."

"I know."

"The whole land called me ungrateful. People are influenced very easily. And they all want to be the ones to straighten people out ... they feel better about themselves when someone else is the problem. They started looking down on me ... I became a collective problem ... I always wondered how people can share the same perceptions about you without even knowing you."

"It's because we all have problems ... that's what we have in common ... and when we find a person or a thing to dump all our issues ... to make them our punching bag, we don't think any further because we all want to release the burden we are carrying."

I touched her back and tried to hug her.

"I was all alone ... but when you came it gave me light ... I know I can trust you."

She accepted the hug. I felt bad about questioning her. I had been right about her.

I stopped coughing, I realized I didn't have time to be weak. I had to protect her. Listening to her took me back when I was just a young woman listening to all the stories of our land and it imprinted an anger inside of me that I would never be able to silence. I had to go back to my son but before that I had to make sure Harlow was safe. When you become an angry woman, you always have an annoyed demeanor because you are fighting your thoughts, you are not in a war against the world, but against your demons. You could be having a good day and then you think about everything you have experienced or witnessed, and it instantly changes your mood.

Chapter 5

The plates of the house and the weak windows reinforced by wooden boards were losing the war. Everything was trembling.

I opened the fly net, and I tried not to step on Adowa. She was sleeping on the floor, she said that after prison, it became her favorite place. She noticed me and grabbed my leg by the calves.

"What's happening?"

"I don't know. Let's go check."

There was no way to peek from the windows because they were completely covered. After speaking to Harlow, I understood why she was so careful. Harlow and Theo joined us. We stepped outside and we almost slipped on the muddy ground. It was raining! Our eyes filled with rainwater, and we could hardly see. The clouds grew dark and impatient.

We could hear Mahamba's voice. He was on the roof of his house with all the leaders. He announced the rain, like he had some mystical power that ordered the weather.

"There is time to wait and time to prepare ... he who believes prepares himself," he shouted.

We all looked up. He was delighted; everything was going

according to his plan. The Elikyans were content as well, looking at him, praising him, with the same admiration that Harlow did not feel. The people were wearing old, crumpled and torn clothes, like the ones we used to donate to the church, or the faulty ones Aunt Noli would get rid of. They opened their mouths, trying to taste the water, like they couldn't believe it. We couldn't hear Mahamba properly because the people were so loud and excited.

Mahamba declared, "Now it's growing season. We need time for the crops to grow ... I would like to ask you my dear Elikyans to start 40 days of fasting to thank us for remaining hopeful.".

What? 40 days of fasting? These people were already dying. I looked over to Harlow trying to see how she felt about this, and her demeanor confirmed that this was another scam.

Theo disappeared, knowing him, he was probably finding ways to store the water. Adowa was celebrating the rain, thinking it mean we were about to go home. She started dancing, doing the 'Adowa dance' which we had named on the black side. She would move around and gently put her hands in motion. Her hands were softly doing different things, while her legs were working together but doing a set of moves that I couldn't follow though everyone else was imitating them. It was very hard for me to follow dance steps; my body was stiff. Everyone gathered around Adowa; they were completely unbothered by Mahamba's announcement. People lack common sense and that's not because of not having access to books and not learning how to read – it's because common sense is for the brave. The Elikyans enjoyed not having to think because thinking leads you to become bitter and resentful.

I looked up at the leaders and I studied each face, especially Cunene, Namibe and Benguela, to see if they would give me a clue of what was behind this. They were on professional mode, cold and not expressing their feelings about Mahamba's decision.

These people wouldn't survive fasting. Was it possible that we were too late, Mahamba's stock of food was completely finished, and he couldn't share that information? If he did it would make him look like he lost control? I started wondering.

They all danced with Adowa, and so did some of the animals. I didn't know most of their names, I only remember Aunt Noli calling men 'pigs', mom and dad calling black people 'dogs', and black people always talking about chickens. They were all over the place, stepping on my toes, and passing in between people's legs. They smelled like the dirt from belly buttons, and they gave me chills. To be honest, I was afraid of animals. If we couldn't trust people, who we could have a conversation with, how could we trust humans those we couldn't communicate understand?.

The next day, Mahamba asked us to meet him at the farms. It was disturbingly hot and where my clothes touched my skin they burned me. There were puddles of water everywhere and people were drinking from them. I couldn't stop scratching myself because there were now bugs everywhere – different kinds that I never seen, some flying, and some trying to crawl over my body. They had tiny, lightweight wings. You could barely see them, but you could hear them, and the noise made me constantly slap my own ear. I could feel whenever red flies were coming, I guess that was my superpower now since I didn't have the dreams anymore. Growing up I heard so many stories about them and how deadly they were to black people. I was raised with egotistical values that told me that I was immune to them. Adowa would look at me and laugh; she knew I wasn't made for this environment. I wasn't coping, and my health was slowly deteriorating. The people always seemed to cope with their adversities, but this rain gave them the real hope everyone from Elikya had been preaching. When we arrived, Mahamba was already there patiently waiting with Cunene, Namibe and Huila.

"Jodi, Theo, and Adowa, we want to thank you for the work you have done," Mahamba started.

I felt relief, I was praying he was going to say we were free to go.

"Well, we didn't have a choice." Theo was also not coping well, and it was starting to show.

"It will take around 40 days for the crops to grow. We will use this time to reflect and to thank our land for giving us another chance." He looked around to see the work we had done.

"These people won't make 40 days without food ... they are already struggling." Theo wasn't accepting this bull.

"When you are in the dark and you see light, even though it's a tiny light ... it gives you hope to continue ... They will be blessed after the 40 days." He continued his rant of hope.

I had never thought that people were capable of using something like food as a way to threaten others, something that was given to us by the divine being.

"They are your people ... You decide! We have done everything you asked, and now we need to go back."

Theo held me and Adowa, and it appeared that he had forgotten about Gunda.

"What about Gunda?" Adowa was worried.

Mahamba took forever to answer her. I always wondered if people who do that are digesting the question or preparing a lie.

91

"Gunda will still stand on Babemba and face the consequences of his actions."

"Okay ... and when will this take place?"

Theo was losing his patience.

"After the 40 days," Mahamba replied.

Was he going to starve us to the point that we couldn't think clearly and wouldn't be able to defend Gunda?

"Mahamba ... I understand the importance of fasting, but we won't make it," I pleaded.

"Fasting is spiritual, its discipline. It's the way we thank earth for everything. It's gratitude. It develops strength. You will feel rejuvenated after."

He made a gesture like he was worshiping his body. He was a slim man always covered with loose and heavy clothes. When he mentioned 'gratitude' I thought about Harlow. Then my mind took me 20 years ago, when Juvey was fasting because Dad ordered her to, and I thought she had misbehaved or something, but Dad said it was for her to resist temptation. It just crossed my mind that at the time Juvey was probably already pregnant and my dad had wanted her to lose the baby. I almost threw up. Theo noticing how this was affecting me, held me. Cunene made a sign for me to take it easy, he nodded with his head for us to trust him.

"Jodi can't make it for 40 days ... We are tired ... We are weak." Theo continued to hold me.

"Tomorrow, I will host you at my home. Come ... Harlow can also join us."

Mahamba turned around and left with his people. When he mentioned her, he gave me a weird look implying that he was aware of how close we were. I wasn't sure what he meant by 'host'.

At home, we informed Harlow about the invitation. She was skeptical and didn't seem excited. I guess thinking about food didn't make her ecstatic; she described the event as something she genuinely despised. She shared with us that they usually hosted a banquet at the leader's house, with a lot of food being served. She told us that from time to time they would organize a formal gathering with all the leaders, and they would invite new arrived guests from another land or people they would try to convince to do something. She didn't fall for either of his traps.

The balmy weather was making me feel weak and it was affecting my vision. I felt constantly dizzy, and I always had to lean into someone. Theo took me to my room, and we left Adowa and Harlow talking about a plan to teach the kids in the land how to read. I wasn't sure how they were going to teach starving kids anything. I wondered how they would concentrate, memorize, or be in the mood to learn anything. I was being critical about everything because this hope culture was a scam. I was tired of people in power selling dreams to the people. Vince always wanted me to see life for what it was and what people were capable of, and I did. Vince would be proud of how bitter I had become.

"Hey ... Don't think about it too much ... We will come up with something." Theo held my head like he was about to kiss me.

"I am just tired of everything." I started scratching my red arm reacting from all the insects that wanted to try white blood.

"It will be over soon," he promised but it was a weak promise.

He started inspecting my arm and then dared to carefully touch it. I felt an instant sexual desire to be touched in other places.

"Theo ... I think you should go back home ... Your family is waiting for you ... I don't have a good feeling about this ... Caleb needs you."

It sounded just like his weak promise. It was baseless. I didn't want Theo to go. I had enjoyed the last few days because I had been next to him every minute.

"I can't ... I can't leave you ... I lost you once ... I am not going to lose you again."

He pulled himself away from me and was ready to head to the door. I knew exactly what he meant but I wasn't ready to listen to that. It has been almost 20 years; how could he still feel the same? How was it possible? It was possible because I felt the same.

"Wait." I held his arm and pulled him closer to me.

"Jodi."

The way he said my name was just different. Theo always brought me back to before everything. Like every bad thing just faded away with Theo, I was no longer this warrior. I was just a girl with parents and a sister.

He pulled away, but I pushed him closer to me. He was confused, he hadn't even considered this. They say men walk around suffering from lust, but I don't think Theo had thought about that. I think he would trade lust with me for taking care of me any time. I wanted him, I longed for this. It had been a long time since I had been in a bed with a man. I kissed him in a clumsy way like I had be meaning to do for days. My arms were awkwardly moving and trying to grab his face the best way to feel his tongue. I don't remember how his kiss felt, to be honest I don't remember how it felt to kiss anymore. He kept looking at my arm with the scratches and holding me, because I was still dizzy, but I didn't care about my health. He finally gave up trying to fight me and pulled me back again and I decided that he was going to take control.

94

Since I was kind of weak, he let me rest; I didn't have to move a finger. He was going to do everything. Maybe that's what I needed. He uncovered my light blue dress – borrowed from Harlow – and placed it on my belly. It was dark, I don't think he could see anything, but he handled everything like he knew my body, like I was still his and I still had a sixteen-year old's body. He pulled down my white lace panties which I had been washing every single day since this life of being a soldier doesn't allow you to pack. He gently kissed my pubes and the whole groin area, he then proceeded to dive little deeper, and inserted his tongue. I felt the coarse hair of his beard rubbing my rough pubes. His blond beard hair got mixed with mine, making knots. I wasn't sure what he was doing but I wasn't scared, I never felt scared around Theo, nothing could happen to me if Theo was around.

With Vince, everything had always been so aggressive and quick because we had not been safe; anyone could have shown up at the house with news that would completely shift the mood.

Now, I could literally feel what was happening there, like that organ of my body became my brain, like my head was not my head anymore, like my head was now my private part, which was not private anymore, because he had access to it. He was touching me like he owned me, like he always did, and he wasn't scared of claiming me. He kept sucking my pelvic skin in a way that meant I couldn't think clearly anymore; my brain stopped functioning.

I wanted to talk but the words wouldn't come out properly. I was making a weird noise like I was struggling to breath, like he had covered and taped my mouth. All of a sudden, my organs' responsibilities and functions were all over the place. I wanted to speak with my vulva, but it was stranded. He then paused, which I wanted to beg him not to, but I was afraid he wasn't able

95

to breathe, and he blew gently air into it, like he puffed dark plants, like he was doing mouth to mouth resuscitation to my lady parts. I felt a breeze in there, then I felt my feet dancing.

The whole time, his eyes were on me, and I wondered how he was able to keep his mouth down then and focus on my face, like he wanted to notice every feeling he was provoking. Each step of the process, he looked into my eyes, to see if I was okay.

He started crawling my body with his head like he was a snake. I remembered that animal because when Mirror was still a baby, Vince had killed every single of them in the area to protect his son. I couldn't think about Vince now, I had to focus on Theo. The man who had never stopped loving me.

His head reached my boobs, I don't know if he remembered them; they were one of things that changed the most on my body. He sucked my nipple, while still looking at me, and I tried so hard to keep my face still, to not give into sensation. I felt my cheekbones relaxing, like my wrinkles smoothed. Where did Theo learn this? Where did people learn these things?

He held me with his two arms under my armpit and lifted me a bit. I didn't want to do any work, I just wanted to watch him do whatever he wanted with me. He wasn't talking or asking questions, he was going to do whatever he wanted.

He started kissing my whole face, and then leaned to my lips, while his hands touched my thighs and my timid butt. He had removed my whole dress by then, I hadn't even noticed. The more he touched me, the more our groins got closer to the point that I wanted to say something, but it wasn't necessary because he could feel every reaction.

He took all of his clothes off. I think he secretly wanted me to do it, but I wasn't able to, I was possessed with something that didn't allow me to move.

96

He held my face and wanted me to concentrate on his face, so he could fill me up. His kisses didn't allow me to process each movement of pleasure; I was overwhelmed with sensations. We heard the noise of rain falling. He looked at me and smiled, relived that it was another day of rain. The rain was getting aggressive, and he looked to me to see if I was scared. My eyes were focused on the closed windows. He touched my hands to show me everything was okay but never stopped riding. It felt good. My breathing was slowly calming down, just like the rain. Everything went silent but he was still inside of me, making very slow and gentle movements, and reading every expression of my face, trying to see if I was enjoying it. I was.

What just happened? I asked myself. Making love to him had been sincere, calm, silent, and everlasting. I couldn't sleep; I relived that moment many times before I fell asleep. I wanted to make sure I could memorize every movement and feeling, so, whenever I would go through something, I could think about it, and it would erase any dark thoughts.

I remembered Pastor Philips shaming women for enjoying making love, like it was a sin. If They allowed us to feel that we should enjoy it and not shame people. For years, I didn't think about it because I had bigger problems, but I can't say I didn't miss it.

The next day, the leaders sent us clothes to wear. They were in bright colors, and the patterns expressed some kind of message and identity. Harlow told us that before Mahamba used them as puppets, the clothing used to be chosen based on the group of people they represented in order for every clan to have a voice and leadership. She also told me stories of each community: in certain tribes when a man died his widow was forced to marry one of his relatives to keep the possessions; others where a newlywed bride was kept in the kitchen by the husband's family for one week in order for her to become fat and she could only step out to bath, she was not allowed to see anyone; how a man would only become a man if he stole an animal from another group; different groups used to have different ways to handle the dowry, the taller the women the more expensive; and she also shared different practices of circumcision. I thought about Mirror. I had never allowed anyone to see my child naked, other than me. Harlow told me that they did the same practice to women to prevent them for feeling pleasure, because it would make them promiscuous at an early age. She also shared how they would kill people born with a disability or any abnormality, but this practice had been instantly abolished in order to keep Elikya culture of inclusivity. She added that in some tribes, a women would be asked to cook only with her head, without using her hands, to show that she would be able to cook for her husband even if she lost her limbs. When the stories were too dark, and especially about women, I asked her to stop.

Theo was acting even more protective; he couldn't leave me alone for one minute. And I can't say I didn't enjoy it. No matter how old you are, you become a little girl when it comes to love.

I missed my walks when I was with him, I missed how I talked ... you change so much about yourself to accommodate people and not bother them, then you realize that their conclusion about you wasn't really about you, it was an assumption that they use to categorize people that they can't stand.

Every time I went to the leaders' house, I was introduced to a new room. They took us downstairs, to a basement that looked dark from the stairs, but when we reached we were welcomed by shea candles everywhere and loud laughs from the leaders. Luanda was playing an instrument that I didn't recognize; he held it like a baby and used his fingers to make sounds. It made me think about Theo's fingers inside of me. I have survived years without it, but now I don't think I can go any day without being intimate with this man.

The table was long and narrow. The places were close together and we sat looking directly into each other's eyes. I couldn't pretend I was okay with this. I haven't been to something so formal since I was a fully white girl. They were all wearing special fabric that Aunt Noli would definitely love – it was heavy, and I could tell that you would need to have a lot of food to trade for it. I guess that's where they spent all the food supplies. However, there was so much food in front of me that I didn't think that Mahamba's stock was ending any time soon.

I recognized some animals, animals in format of food, but they still had a strong odor. The air was heavy with spices. I was getting nauseous; I wasn't sure if it was the food itself or the hypocrisy. The fasting didn't include us, it was only for the people. Even the culture of not killing animals was only for the common Elikyas – the leaders were killing animals to feed themselves. I remember Dad saying that they were going to start collecting possessions from the people to help the land. I recall him using big words in conversations with other lawyers, saying 'a compulsory contribution, levied by us'. I didn't have to be grown to know it was faulty and this whole façade reminded me of that scam.

Most of them were eating like animals. The crumbs would fall all over their exorbitant clothes and onto the table. I noticed

99

Moxico's face; he had deep scratch marks, like they were burnt onto his face, in patterned designs. I wondered if they were permanent. Harlow had told me about it earlier, but I just couldn't bear to hear any more atrocity.

I looked over Adowa, she was behaving like them, eating like it was her last meal. I think she believed that this dinner was the last dinner before fasting, but I knew the fasting didn't apply for some, and us being part of that privileged group would cost us, maybe our friend's life. Theo was more cautious, he was eating and smelling the food, trying to make sure it wasn't poisoned. I could tell he wasn't sure what was happening, but he wanted to be well fed for whatever was coming. Harlow barely touched the food, or she wanted to seem like she wasn't touching it, but I caught her hiding some scraps under her skirt. What was she up to?

Theo was sitting next to me and made a sign with his eyes for me to eat, he pointed specifically at some yellowish spicy rice that smelled so strong that you could eat it with your nose. I wanted to focus on the leaders and try to gather more information, but the music was loud, and I couldn't hear them properly. I looked over to Mahamba and he made a sign for me to eat, then over to Cunene who was enjoying the food but not in the same happy mood as the others, like Namibe and Huila. Benguela wasn't eating much, she was picky with her selection, I guess. There were veggies everywhere which was alarming because they were fresh, where had they come from? I kept looking at Harlow to give me answers and explain the luxury in front of me, but she was too busy stealing. I could smell her; she had taken pieces of chicken and roasted potatoes. I bent to her ear, and I whispered what was she doing. She didn't answer and continued grabbing everything she could.

The noise from the forks being thrown around was louder than the symphony Luanda was trying to make. Some were using forks, other were trying but failing, and the majority were relying on their hands. They were licking their fingers and sucking the meat stuck in their nails. I wanted to throw up. Theo kept looking at me, trying to read me just like last night, trying to see every reaction in my face but I was trying my best to keep the composure and act like I was okay with this villainy. I thought about Gunda, did he have access to food? I got lost in my thoughts and I didn't notice when Harlow stepped out. I discreetly left the room, hoping no one noticed (except Theo, because he was my shadow now). I got lost trying to find the exit, there were so many rooms filled with provisions, like they were stocking and preparing for a season of scarcity.

I walked around looking for Harlow. I followed the smell of food and I found her at some house door, in a worst state then hers. She handed some food to a lady who looked like a gypsy but without the will to dance anymore. It wasn't normal to see a gypsy with a weak spirit. Mom used to tell me that they were the best dancers, and musicians, and that some worked at the circus. Mom said that before she had us she had wanted to run away with the circus. I knew that gypsies were also good with animals, especially horses. I don't think I had ever seen a horse before. Vince said they were used a long time ago for the wars.

Harlow noticed me spying on her. I could tell the food was heavy because she was walking slowly, but she still managed to knock many doors. I noticed she was covering her patches, which continued to spread, so as not to scare people. The first time I saw her, I had thought she was beautiful, and I was relieved that she was happy with her conditions, which made me feel hopeful for my son. But now, seeing her stealing food from the privileged to give to those in need, beautiful wasn't enough to describe her. I understand now how Aunt Noli fell for a woman.

"You need to go back ... They will notice you left." Harlow continued to walk and finish her generous task.

"They won't notice ... they are too busy enjoying the perks of greed."

"Okay, but don't follow me ... you might scare them ... they are very suspicious," Harlow warned me.

"Wait ... I need to understand." I held her arm from the back.

"What you need to understand Jodi? You always need to understand everything. There's nothing to understand here?" She freed her arms and continued walking.

"These people hate you. They shamed you. They agreed with opinions about you without even knowing you ... and you still help them?" I was angry, my anger started earlier at the dinner, and I had to find some way to release it. Whenever we see an act of kindness, we always try to understand it and test it because it has become so rare. She turned to me and smiled, and then proceeded to continue her good deeds.

"Harlow." I tried to get an answer out of her. I wasn't sure what I wanted to hear.

"What do you want from me? That's all I know ... They don't know any better, but I do."

She was almost crying, she continued walking door to door.

I realized that people are lazy, they don't want to see the truth if it is not accepted by the majority. It's like reading a book, it takes time, but it's easier to judge the cover.

"They exclude you ... they don't respect you ... but I do ... I see you." I kept following her and trying to talk to her.

"What is respect? People always talk about respect ... respect ... respect ... they respect Mahamba, is that the kind respect you want? A blind servitude? They can treat me whatever they want ... What they did to me caused them more hurt in them than me." Her words were firm. She paused, turned, and faced me with conviction. I realized she was the legendary hero we used to talk about on the black side. We were all inspired by this story, about someone who would steal from wealthy and give to the poor, but we always thought it was a man.

I felt drops of water in my eyes, I looked at the sky and saw that it was getting ready to rain, just like we plotted – to be able to cultivate. Harlow didn't stop, she was going to finish delivering the food at all costs, so I followed her. The rain became intense, more aggressive than the previous night. She finished delivering the food before it became too wet. I held her and I told her she had done good, but it was time to go.

We waited a bit, but the rain wasn't stopping; the sky was angry. There were flashes of lighting visible in between the rain-bearing cloud. The sky was making loud noises, like it was warning that something was about to happen. We found shelter on the porch of one of the houses. I could feel the metal and steel fighting the rain. The noise was scaring us, but we sat firm waiting for it stop. I don't think I had ever witnessed anything like that. It felt like someone shouting at us, but it was just nature fighting an enemy that we didn't know anything about. This rain wasn't almighty; it was devastating and deadly. When it finally calmed down, we headed home with our heavy clothes soaked in water. My cough was back, and I couldn't breathe properly.

I stayed in bed for a few days. Theo was furious about what had happened that day and since then I couldn't move without his permission.

In the mornings, I could hear Benguela bringing books to Adowa and Harlow so they could start their mission. They were going to every home to teach the children how to read. Adowa had won them over after the dance. I enjoyed seeing her being liked and not being feared. I heard Benguela preparing them on how to convince the parents. She instructed them to say that it was Mahamba's idea and after the 40 days, they would host a ceremony, inviting all of the Elikyans and this would be a gift to Mahamba, in his honor. I wouldn't buy that, but I guess they did. The thing about shady people is that there is always a scam and sometimes to dethrone them you need to resort to the same ways they play. I wonder how he could trust his servants, especially all eighteen; they were probably hard to control. There is always someone who will revolt against authority.

At night, Theo would check on me, to see if I was strong enough to withstand his rain. I wanted to feel his precipitation, his raindrops inside of me, undergo his wet weather, and experience a sprinkle of his magic. Outside, the rains never stopped, I would fall asleep with the noise and wake up with the earthy smell that would make me miss farming, but I was too weak to go back. It had been a few weeks, there was probably something already growing.

Chapter 6

Mahamba asked us to meet him at the plantations. He wanted to see how everything was going. Theo told me that the time to grow the crops depended on the types of seeds, so we distributed and divided the areas according to the seeds. We did a good job; the soil was prepared, and we managed to level it and make it lighter. I missed sowing the seeds. I didn't realize how much we had worked; it was a wide plantation. In math, I was told that we could count the space, but I couldn't remember how to.

Unfortunately, the rainwater carried away some of the soil, and it caused some kind of erosion. I studied Mahamba's reaction to see if he was going to say something, but he always acted like his plans were under control. There were areas where the rain had infiltrated the soil, and this had been possible because of the plant's roots. The smell was more pleasant than the dry smell of dead plants and animal corpses. But it was hotter than before, so hot that you could see waves moving in the air; it made my vision blurry.

Mahamba kept going around the plantation, and ordered Malanje, Bengo, Lunda- Sul, Lunda-Norte, and Kwanza-Sul to study the vegetation. I don't know how I memorized their names. I guess how violent they were when they had grabbed the food had left an imprint on my mind. I couldn't forget their scarred hands touching the food like it was the soil. I could still smell them from afar. I wondered where Cunene, Namibe and Huila were, I had not seen them in a while. At the dinner, they had all kept quiet, especially Huila. Harlow shared that women usually don't talk much when there is man at the table.

Theo looked over to the sky. The colors were changing from baby blue to the kind of blue that Zaire sometimes paints his face. We could see something that looked like tree trunks in the sky, I didn't know what to call it, but it was scary. I looked over to Theo to see if he knew but he seemed as lost as I was. This time the rain didn't start slowly, like the way Theo crawled over my body, it didn't waste time showing its rage. We tried to scream and make a sign for the leaders to join us running back to the settlement. Theo held my hand and pulled me, forcing me to run faster, while the leaders struggled to run in their heavy royal attire.

Inside the community everything was wide open, except the houses, but the houses were just as weak as the residents. We ran to Harlow's house, the roof was collapsing, and the metal was fighting against the rain. Every different type of house, whether constructed of sand, concrete or bricks, were giving up the fight. However, the leaders' house remained untouched and stubborn, protected by its cement binder.

The rain never stopped and there was no way to hid. It kept pouring in an aggressive way, you couldn't see anything clearly. The leaders reached their houses and entered without looking back. They had soggy clothes and selfish eyes, ignoring what was happening around. I was shaking, I could feel my muscles contracting and my raised hair follicles forced my pores to close.

"Jodi, let's go inside … we can't do anything about it." Theo pulled me into the door.

"No! We need to do something!"

I went back outside, started pulling people and directing them to the leaders' house. It was the only safe place. Uíge heard the noise and opened the door. His eyes were confused, he wasn't sure if he was allowed to let us in. We pushed him over and we all slid in. I was holding two little girls and Theo was helping their parents. We placed them inside the entrance where the rain was bleeding on the walls, but it wasn't dripping. I ran back outside to get the rest of the people; the water reached my knees and I had to grab anything I could to keep my balance and I leaned against the remains of the other houses. I made a sign for people to enter the leaders' house. Meanwhile, Mahamba and the others were on the rooftop watching us. The other leaders started going downstairs, one by one, to receive the people.

My hair slapped my face because the wind was so strong. I kept looking for children under the remains of the houses. I was stepping carefully, afraid of finding a brick, or the leg of a baby. I looked over to a cream-colored house now dark with water stains. I saw a family standing on their roof tiles.

The water never stopped. It was almost ankle-deep. I wondered what the limit was. What was happening? I hadn't seen anything like it in my life. It felt like the earth was resentful and wanted to punish us. I kept hearing people screaming and children crying. Everyone was in panic. The whole thing felt like a dance, where you look at people's moves and try to learn in the moment. I saw people climb the houses trying to reach the roof like the others. Some managed, but others slipped instantly. I grabbed as many people as possible, and I kept looking back to see if Theo was okay.

"Jodi!! We did enough!!! Let's go!!" he shouted.

He had grabbed an older woman who was hanging from the grids of her house. I saw the wood that people would use to protect their windows floating. I grabbed a few pieces, and I started paddling. This was the end. I couldn't imagine anything worse than this. I thought about that day when I offered myself to the ocean.

"*For I know the plans I have for you ...Plans to prosper you and not to harm you, plans to give you hope and a future.*" I was whispering to myself.

"Jodi! Jodi! Let's go!" Theo grabbed me and started shaking me. He knew my mind was somewhere else. I felt like I had lived this before. Sometimes I feel like we live in a cycle, and we will experience the same thing repeatedly. I didn't fight him, and I let him guide me just like the water. I looked up and I saw Mahamba, still looking at us. I couldn't tell what was going through his mind.

"Where are Adowa and Harlow?"

I was about to step inside onto the leaders' house's slippery floor when I realized I had forgotten them. I wanted to go back outside but Theo stopped me.

"They are fine."

He pulled me back and held me in my drenched clothes. Water from his hair dripped onto my face.

The house was packed with Elikyans, and we couldn't even move. They were sitting on the floor, on the stairs, and anywhere they could fit. We kept waiting for Mahamba to come and say something, but he didn't. His silence was scarier than the suspicious peace that came after the rain. Theo and Cunene were walking around trying to keep people calm. His expression told me he knew what happened. I remember that when he was working on his car, he used to talk about an electrical storm or lighting. The rain had an acoustic effect, the same consistent sound of water pouring fast for a while and then a stronger sound that reminded me of the engine that would make Theo's car start working.

"Mahamba is calling you." Cabinda, completely dry with no soggy clothes, found me in between the mourners of the rain.

I could easily feel the breath of the person next to me because we were squeezed so close. I followed him upstairs and Theo did the same. On the rooftop, Mahamba was still looking at the settlement and his back was turned. I saw Harlow and Adowa sitting patiently, not wet like me and Theo, but definitely more so than Mahamba. I was surprised but relived to see them (they later shared that they had been stranded in one of the houses where they went to teach). I didn't know what this encounter with Mahamba meant but I didn't have a good feeling, the atmosphere was as frightening as the rain.

"I can see you all are safe." Mahamba turned to face the four of us. Had we been caught? I tried to see if Benguela was nearby to give me a sign of what was this about.

"Yes. Just like you." Theo observed his dry clothes.

"I have to admit ... I am impressed ... I haven't seen such bravery, and courage in a long time." He looked over to Harlow, implying that she had done something like this in the past.

"It was the least we could do." I emphasized. I didn't care about his mind games.

"I guess I am running out of thank yous ... There is so much to thank you for." He walked around with his head down.

"No need ... we just want to go home." Theo's hands were

109

shaking.

"And you will ... We would never keep you against your will," Mahamba stated.

Adowa was about to answer when I touched her hand. She decided to express her discomfort by scratching her wet hair. Whenever her hair was wet it would shrink so much that she would look like she had had a haircut.

"But you are!" Harlow's lips were shaking like she was scared.

What was happening? I was trying to read the room. She would usually avoid talking to him and he did the same, but something was really upsetting her.

"Whatever happened today can't happen again ... I won't tolerate my people fighting for their lives ... We don't want this witchcraft here." He looked directly to Adowa. Witchcraft? Was he calling her a witch.

"What?" Harlow started laughing, it was so uncomfortable that we all looked at each other trying to understand what was happening.

"You people came here with these things – these magic things. You did this!" He was walking around and pointing at the damage outside. I had never seen him so unhinged; he always seemed he had everything under control.

"With all respect sir ... It's just a positive thinking ... It's a mantra," Adowa intervened. Her voice was low and calm, but she was a bit shaky, maybe because of the weather, I hoped. I knew how Mahamba comments would deeply impact her since she had been called a witch before.

"I don't care what it is. Make it stop! I order you!" He started screaming like a lunatic, throwing his long and heavy wardrobe around, like he wanted to undress himself. It was pathetic.

"I think we should concentrate on the losses and find out if

110

anyone has been injured or lost their lives." Theo moved his hands, trying to reach Mahamba, in an attempt to calm him down.

"No one passed way," Harlow revealed. She had arrived here when she was very young, and she knew everyone.

"Make it stop, I order you!" He ignored Harlow and looked straight at Adowa.

Adowa was getting uncomfortable; she had good intentions. The people here really loved her. She hadn't experienced that kind of love in a long time.

"You are so obsessed with control ... but you can't control everything ... This is nature ... We lived with years of drought and then the rain came. It changed everything. You have been polluting this land for years. Doing whatever it pleases you. The earth is angry." Harlow was laughing between her words, but still they held so much relevance.

Mahamba finally faced her. He couldn't read her, but he knew we were up to something.

"Whatever it is ... we don't want it here!" He restored his calmness. He pretended that he knew what we were hiding but his unbalanced demeanor undermined him.

The other leaders made us a sign that it was time to go.

Harlow was on her way to the stairs, when she looked back and quoted someone. "Once a wise man said, 'You pray for rain, you gotta deal with the mud too'."

I wasn't sure who the person was, but I knew I heard it before. I realized that it wasn't about them not respecting her, they were actually scared of her. When people exude confidence, a self-belief that keeps them going, it upsets people around them.

"I said that?" Mahamba responded. It was the first time that he had spoken to her directly.

"I said a wise man."

Harlow clearly annoyed every hair of Mahamba's body. I looked to the reactions of the leaders; some were trying to hold their laughs. Others were giving her angry looks, which she ignored. Harlow was a true hero, not like me. I was born into a family and a race that gave me an advantage; I was privileged. I knew I could do damage, and nothing could happen to a white girl at the time. Maybe that's why Vince choose me. He knew the whites couldn't win against themselves.

On the way back, Benguela decided to accompany us. She shared the story of the eighteen leaders with us. I had always been intrigued about the number. Years ago, even before Harlow arrived, there were a group of eighteen people, many of them poets and writers, who were accused of plotting to overthrow the leader of the land – Mahamba's grandfather. The family had been ruling Elikya for a hundred years, and people were tired. These eighteen rebels were from different clans and lineages but were working together to fight for their people. They were writing a book exposing what Mahamba's family was doing to the people. I guess that's where Vince took inspiration. They were sent to prison but after many negotiations, they became an auxiliary support to the sovereign family.

It didn't rain for a few days, which left us at ease. The leaders would invite us for a banquet sometimes, which was another way to control us. The fasting wasn't so bad, I actually felt younger and lighter. Food sometimes made me feel overwhelmed, and it constantly affected my mood. Fasting was peaceful and allowed me to be control of my body. I would feel fatigue, and I could sense the blood inside of me missing something. My arms would itch sometimes, like the blood needed support to keep me alive. Still, I didn't miss meals that much, there was something else that became my subsistence: I longed for Theo.

I wanted to make love to Theo every single day, hour, and minute. I don't know how I had survived all those years without it. I felt angry about being deprived of it all these years. It wasn't just the pleasure; it was about how safe I felt with him when he was doing it and how confident he was when he was touching me.

Making love to Vince had been aggressive; I am not even sure if I ever enjoyed it or if I was just doing for the sake of passing time and to forget I had abandoned my family because of him. Making love to Theo was about me, what I wanted, what made me feel good. Vince never looked at me when we were doing it, he would choose certain love positions where he didn't face me, maybe he wasn't attracted to me, or maybe he was embarrassed. Perhaps because of my age or race? Whatever it was, I felt used all the time, either for love or for war. I think Vince was only aroused by me when we were actually doing it. Theo would look at me and I could tell that this man couldn't wait to grab me. I felt it every time I saw him. I wanted to lie to myself, but it was so evident. For years, I had avoided him because I could tell he wanted to plant seeds of pleasure in me, and finally we were doing it.

I was sitting in Theo's lap; it felt like I was sixteen again. He held me like I was this precious thing. He grabbed my hairy neck with all the hair that wouldn't make it to my weak ponytail, because it was too busy getting entangled with my necklace, the one grandma gave to Juvey. My necklace had seen it all, all those years that I prayed that nothing happened to my child and how I resented myself for fighting a cause that I didn't know anything about. I regretted meeting Vince. Theo pulled my face into his and erased all that regret. I tried to be in the moment, but I couldn't stop comparing him to Vince. Vince had rarely kissed me. I don't remember how it felt but whatever it felt like, it was nothing compared to Theo's warm, caring and long-lasting kisses. I never got tired of kissing him. Even though there was something building in me to want more than kisses, I was never done with kissing him. The sexual tension kept increasing and I almost reached the peak, I felt pressure and persuasion from my genitals to demand more, but before I could ask, he noticed that his pants, damaged by the rain, were wet. The rain had come from me this time; I was all soaked in pleasure. I held him tight, and I gave him a hug. Then, I heard a slight knock on the door, then many knocks at the same time. Theo pushed me away and looked around the living room to sense what was happening. It was raining, it wasn't just me. My bladder was full, like I could pee for hours. It pained him to stop what we were doing and leave me like this, but we had to warn Adowa and Harlow.

Harlow and Adowa were inseparable. They would leave in the morning to teach the children of different families. When they reached home, they would share how difficult it had been, sometimes, to convince the parents. They would knock door to door and sometimes convince them with some food in exchange. Adowa said that sometimes the parents would join because they actually wanted to learn but other times, they would just sit there suspicious.

The rain wasn't aggressive like the other day. It was more a Theo kind of rain, gentle and patient. We didn't know which house they were in. We knocked each door, asking for them.

After the heavy rains, the houses looked like they were about to fall: the plate, the aluminum, the straw: everything was weaker than the residents. The whole town smelled rusty.

We avoided leaving the house because of our last encounter with Mahamba. Harlow and Adowa would sneak out in secret. I was afraid of knocking very hard because the doors looked unstable, like they were made of chaff, straight from the farms.

We stopped at a house with a small ceiling at the entrance, which allowed us to hide. There was a long window with eight divisions and one of them was broken. I heard Adowa's voice. I pulled over to check if it was really her. I saw her, Harlow, and three children, sitting on the floor. Two boys and a girl laying on the ground, holding their necks to pay close attention to Adowa. Their smiles showed that they were thrilled to hear the end of the story which prevented me from disturbing them. Adowa around children was the best Adowa; so likeable. Aunt Noli used to say that there is no such thing as not liking someone, only people we don't know. When we see people in their habitat, with the people they love, with the things they love doing, it's impossible not to like them. The smiles on the children's faces were nothing compared to the sound of pleasure in Adowa's voice. She enjoyed this, a war that she didn't have to fight physically, only with her beautiful mind.

"Adowa and Harlow. It's raining. We need to find a place to hide ... I don't have a good feeling about this," Theo screamed through the door, while observing the clouds.

"Sorry! We got carried away."

Harlow opened the door.

"We can't leave them! Their parents are not here."

Adowa held one of the boys, the little one. "You're right! Let's go!"

I held the girl, and Harlow grabbed the other boy.

We followed Theo. He had a plan; I trusted him, just like I trusted him with my body. We left the village and were going in the direction of the farms. I wasn't sure what he had in mind. The girl was heavy, but I kept holding her like she was Mirror. On the way, I saw my sandals slipping away and the water was cold. We reached the sacred tree, the long and strong branches with rebellious plants protected us from the rain. It was going to be our shelter for the next minutes or hours. The rain was so unpredictable, you couldn't read it or understand it. Adowa climbed the tree with no effort. She offered to receive the children and made sure they were safe. When we were all settled and safe, Theo went back to gather more people. They followed him and populated the tree as much as possible. The more rain, the more people followed Theo's plan. We would receive the kids first and then help the parents clamber up. They were running faster than the rain; they would reach the tree and finally breathe. They breathed deeply to find the strength to push their kids and climb the sacred tree. They couldn't stop breathing and it made the leaves flutter. I knew the tree was strong, but I didn't know it was possible to withstand so many people. I guess it was indeed sacred. We felt safer there than in Mahamba's palace of secrets.

"Enough ... I don't think the tree can take more people," A man shouted to Theo, while giving me his kid to hold.

"We will bring anyone who needs help."

Theo basically told him to shut up. He went back, not running anymore because the water was getting higher, and it didn't allow him to move his legs so freely.

"Look!"

I heard Harlow's voice, pointing at something far away. We

could see the whole land from the tree. I wasn't sure what they were looking at, until I saw Adowa's reaction. Mahamba was on his roof top throwing books away so that the rain would take away the books. I was confused about the meaning of this. Sometimes we need time to process the interpretation of cruel acts.

"He knows," Harlow confirmed.

Benguela had been stealing books for weeks now and Mahamba had caught her. Instead of punishing her, he had decided to destroy all of the books from his own library. Our works and hopes to see the next generation of this land able to read had vanished. I wasn't sure if people noticed what was happening; he did it in a very subtle way. We got the message. I was following the books' route sailing the water. I still had hope we could find a way to save them. They all ended up in the same place, all together, completely damaged. Some would fall right in the rainy floor; others would still count on their pages to try to fly away. A few got stuck on the roof tiles but still they didn't make it.

"The rain is sacred, it does not harm," Adowa affirmed. She wasn't fazed by this.

"The rain is sacred, it does not harm." I heard a tiny voice repeating it. It came from a little girl who had taken classes with them.

"The rain is sacred, it does not harm." Each person repeated this, with trembling voices, fighting the rain and the potential for illnesses like flu.

Then we all said at the same time. The way some kids pronounced the phrase told us that we were on the right path and this land was going to be an educated land.

All the kids looked at Adowa like she was this precious thing; she needed that love.

We were all holding the branches like our lives depended on it and we watched an arch of different colors coming to life in the sky. I didn't know what the name for that was. But if the nature could produce something like that, we would be okay.

The soil was soaking the water and it made ponds. The people gathered outside to drink the water and trying to pick up the pieces of their houses. There was foil, metal sheets, and pallets everywhere. We lifted some to see if anyone was injured, but luckily most people were with us at the sacred tree. I speculated about whether Mahamba had a solution for this.

Harlow had shared that they used to receive many people fleeing their lands because of weather disasters. When she had first explained it, I didn't understand what it meant, until I saw with my own eyes. It was a scary experience, seeing them losing everything, from clothes to furniture.

It was hard to stay clean with all the mud and waste every-where, but the sacred tree remained untouchable, like nothing had happened, like we didn't have the whole population holding onto it.

A day later, when the rain had stopped again, Mahamba told us he wanted to meet to see how the planting was doing. We arrived first and took a look at it. It would take months or even years for this to become an orchard. I could smell the plants growing but even the lettuces and tomatoes, which we were told were going to be available soon, would take months, especially now that the rain was becoming a problem. The leaders needed vegetables in their diets, their breath always smelled like roasted animal meat and their heavy clothes preserved the smell for days.

"This rain is suffocating the plants ... They need to breathe."

Mahamba arrived with Cunene, Namibe and Huila.

"Plants are like people. They won't make it, if it continues to rain like this," Cunene added. He walked around, carefully, trying to not step on the vegetation.

They kept blaming us for the rain.

"They will. They just need fertilization. I can already see them growing, we need to add more fertilizer to make it strong. All the waste that the rain caused, we can gather and use it as manure." Theo dropped down to see them clearly and started touching the little stems that showed that there was something coming from underground. I couldn't see anything, I could only smell germs and bugs.

"We are counting on you to give us a beautiful orchard." Mahamba smiled, the same smile I had seen when he had been getting rid of the books.

One thing I had learned in this life was to be civil with evil. I never thought I would finally grasp how to have grace to be pleasant to someone who I knew was not being fair. Juvey shared with me that at the saloon, they did awful things to her, but they would always smile and pretend everything was fine. They labeled her as difficult. Juvey was the easiest person I knew, so easy to love. I was glad I had never worked a day in my life, except this sentence that I was now serving.

"There's something else I would like to ask you." He looked at the demolished houses in town.

"All ears." Theo stopped touching the soil, shook the dust from his hands and faced Mahamba.

I was busy trying to protect my face from the flying black

119

beetles. You could barely see their transparent wings but their noise moving through the air was unbearable. The beetle was upset about something; he wanted to fight me. I kept pushing him away from me, but he kept trying to face me.

"A lot of people lost their homes – we need help to rebuild them." Cunene intervened with his tender demeanor to try to suggest, rather than force, us to do another task.

"We are tired ... We have done everything you have asked ... We have a family back home." Theo pulled his hair back. When he mentioned his family, I realized that my fairy tale was about to be over.

"I promise after this, you are free to go." Mahamba turned his back and was ready to go.

"Wait! Under one condition! Gunda waits for his Babemba free ... He is strong, and he can help us." Theo was struggling to stay polite.

"Fair enough." Mahamba looked back, faced me and Adowa for a few seconds, then left.

Huila and Namibe graciously smiled.

I was more aroused by Theo every day, seeing him taking control was exciting, who would think that my white boy was going to become this man.

At night, I felt someone pulling my arm, trying to wake me up. I really hoped it wasn't another crazy rain. The seeds needed peace to grow, and they grew in the dark, at night. I couldn't believe our fate depended on the weather. I used to think that my love for Vince was like the weather: if he was happy, I would instantly be happy too. If he was in a bad mood, it would also affect me. It was always about him: his cause, his fight. I don't ever remember him asking how I felt. I don't think he cared and that's where Theo would always be one step ahead of him. Even living with another woman, he validated my feelings and made me feel heard. Vince was the warmest coldest person I ever met, he had this thing of ignoring people and then all of the sudden, spontaneously surprise them with hugs. However, it wasn't enough for me, I wanted more. I wanted to be kissed every single day, be loved properly, be taking care of.

"Jodi. Wake up."

Adowa shook my arms. I woke up startled, thinking my dreams were back. I didn't have dreams anymore, but I was having these moments of imagining the worst thing that could happen to me. Like I could picture the present moment going wrong. Like when I am plotting, I can picture the grit thrown at me by mistake and my eyes struggling to see. I don't know what to call it, maybe dark 'daydreaming'. I had it when Mirror was a toddler. I could picture many ways that he could hurt himself and I would get goosebumps and scream like a maniac.

"Mirror ... Mirror ... did something happen to Mirror?" My heart was alert. I held her frantically.

"Mirror is okay Jodi ... calm down ..."

"Is it raining again?"

"No. Everything is fine. I have an idea!"

"Tell me." I adjusted myself comfortably on the bed.

"We still have one book." She smiled.

"Really? Which one?" I wasn't following; I was still sleepy.

"The Book."

"Where is it?"

"I left it with Kofi." She looked up trying to remember something. "Tomorrow when we go pick up Gunda I will try to get it back."

I nodded and turned to go back to sleep. I was tired of planning and doing things, I wanted to go home and see my son. I needed to be a good mother for once. I didn't think I was a real mother to him. Mirror had been raised by Vince's people, not me. I felt like I owed Vince since he passed away, so I let the black community take over, do whatever they wanted to him, from baby rituals to washing him with herbs that were meant to purify him from all the evil. I never asked for anything, but I always wanted my aunt to be involved. I missed my mother; I wanted my mother to take care of Mirror too. I didn't care what my mom did or what she knew dad did, I just missed her, sometimes we gotta admit we are not mad at people anymore, our feelings for them are stronger than anything and can heal any lingering feelings.

Chapter 7

"Jodi ... Theo ... Mahamba has instructed us to free Gunda."
Luanda was standing at the stairs that would take us to
the place of confinement. He was accompanied by Bengo
and Cabinda. I always wondered how Mahamba delegated the
tasks. Where the other go? What are they doing when they are
not around?

"He will stand on Babemba and respond for his crimes."
Cabinda was impersonating Mahamba's demeanor.

"And when is that?" Theo blurted out. He was trying to test if
they had all the information regarding Gunda's fate and trying
to see if they would let something slip.

Meanwhile, Adowa managed to sneak inside to get the Book.

"You will know soon," Cabinda replied, facing the stairs to
see Gunda coming out.

We saw two men carrying Gunda, the same ones who had
carried Adowa. They pulled him from the stairs and gently
dropped him on the floor. A foul smell emerged; I wasn't sure
if it came from Gunda or the guards. Later, Adowa told me that
they were keeping the animals inside so they could survive the
rain. Gunda looked at us trying to understand what it mean for

him to be let out. He probably didn't know much about this land its wacko rules. I smiled trying to tell him that it was okay. They handed him to us, and we headed back home with another visitor that Harlow was going to host. She gushed that she had received many people from other lands. She liked to get close to them because she felt alone in this land. With time, after knowing the whole story and getting accustomed to this land's villainy, they would soon distance themselves from her, and find shelter and protection from someone else.

In the morning, we started our new mission. I was getting tired of being told what to do. I didn't think I would last in a submissive marriage. It wasn't as hot as the weather after the rain, or as warm as the dry season, it was another kind of warmth: like the precious sun was there but you could feel a breeze coming, akin to the sensation you feel right after washing your arse, like you feel your body entirely cleaned by a soft wind.

There were broken tiles and glass on the floor. I had to walk carefully, but I had Theo to show me the way. The houses got mixed up in a heap of damaged stuff. You couldn't tell what belonged to which house. Theo and Gunda were uncovering things and trying to see what was under that mess.

We started cleaning at a house that belonged to Mahamba's nephew, and we looked for things that we could still use. I held a broomstick and concentrated on removing all the dust from all demolished objects. Sweeping was the only thing I could think of doing – all of the other things were dangerous, and I would end up hurt.

Mahamba had told us to gather up personal belongings – I wondered what he was going to do with them. I guessed that was why he had sent Cunene and Namibe; to collect people's belongings. It was nice to work with them again. Huila had been spared and I wished I had the same option. Instead, he said that Harlow could join us this time. I was glad because it was a lot of work and we needed an extra pair of hands, but, knowing this man, it was a punishment for her feisty words the other day.

Adowa was barefoot, like always, so Gunda told her to stay away from the mess and find something to do. She didn't want to be there; I think she missed teaching. This thing was taking a toll on her because she had finally found something she enjoyed. She recounted that Kofi used to read the Book to her and she was delighted to be able to bring the same joy to the kids. It was undeniable that they missed her, whenever we would walk into town, they would run to her.

"*Beat me, hate me ... You can never break me ... will me, thrill me ... You can never kill me,*" Harlow was singing, while walking through the ruins. I followed her trying to hear the lyrics. I had heard the words before. When I had wanted to understand Mirror's condition, I had been told about a man in a black land who had been accused of wanting to be white. People were not familiar with the condition, they didn't understand him, they thought he had brought it on himself.

"Everything is going to be okay ... Adowa has a plan." I tried to cheer up her torn spirit.

"Until when? Until he wakes up and decides to do something else," she mumbled, disappearing into a big bowl of decayed things.

I let her be with her singing. I looked over to Gunda and Theo. They wanted to finish this work as soon possible. Gunda took off his shirt. His skin looked stretched: his bones were visible and there was no fat, just sharpness and structure. I didn't think Gunda had aged all these years; he looked the same. I could picture him occupying his time in prison doing building muscle by facing down on the floor with hands outstretched either perpendicular or parallel to the body then the arms being brought palms down on a right angle at the elbows, and then pushing the body up. I had memories of Vince doing with it with Mirror on his back. I was always afraid he was going to fall. I had never seen Theo doing any exercises, but his calves never aged or weakened. One thing about white men; they had strong calves. While black men, were blessed with a well-built torso just like the branches from the sacred tree.

The Elikyans started joining us to help as we were working on their own homes. It hadn't been our initiative but at least we were doing it. They started to help by picking up the broken plates. People who lost their houses were staying at the leaders' houses, the others who were less affected were working on fixing their own houses.

While we were focusing on the houses, the plants were finally left alone to grow in peace. The rain had disappeared and Mahamba was finally off our backs. He invited us for another banquet at his place. This was one was different; it was a celebration for finishing the 40 days of pretense of fasting. It was more like a festival; the leaders were louder than ever, and they painted their faces in different colors.

I was starting to despise food; I had a constant feeling of wanting to throw up. I looked over at Theo. He was doing the same, smelling it and then passing to me, meaning it was approved. Gunda was eating like he had not eaten in years. I could see the sauce spilling over his hand and over to his arms. The meat on his plate was greyish, and you could tell it wasn't properly cooked, because there was blood mixed with the sauce.

It smelled like cow meat, and I could taste it by just looking at him. Harlow once told me that there used to be certain parts of the cow reserved only for men at traditional ceremonies like weddings and funerals, and others reserved for women. In some tribes, a specific family member is awarded the best piece of the cow depending on the event.

There was music but it was not peaceful and liberating like Harlow's choice of music; it was dramatic and demented. They had different instruments made of wood, making all kinds of sounds. It made me think about the church, my baptism, and even funerals I was forced to go to. I don't think I got along with sounds because I always felt alarmed by something, like something was about to happen.

They served me a beverage and I looked over to Theo to get his approval, but he was busy watching Adowa dancing, so I sipped it all at once. I wondered if he found her attractive, because anyone would. Adowa was the most beautiful woman I had seen my life; I think her beauty got into her head to the point that she became crazy.

She was moving her body, so many moves at once. How could just two legs and two arms do so many things? I couldn't but I wanted to, there was some desire inside of me that I wanted to express. I was too stiff, like I had two left feet. It's like in my mind, I could dance like her, but my body couldn't perform it. The leaders were all around her, smiling, laughing, cheering with their drinks. I don't think anyone could teach me how to dance: it was spiritual, she was born with that. It's like she went to herself, meditated, and gathered all her forces to respond to the rhythm. Her dancing representing everything about her: she was Adowa, she was just simply her, living her own life, knowing who she was, no pretense, no bull ... She once told me that she never prayed before because dancing for her was like praying.

The drink was fermented. They served me another one, the more I sipped the more I wanted to move my body but in a different way. It's like the refreshment woke up something in me. Suddenly, it became hot; there were a few drops of sweat on my chest, so I drank once more. I wanted to take my clothes off and run. I just felt like running, I had been wanting to run for a while now. This wasn't my battle, why was I still here?. Wait, these people came here because of me. I would be a coward if I ran. Thoughts rent my head; my brain was fighting but my body was balmy. I glanced over to Theo, a desire to touch his hair and pull it back came to me, suddenly came.

"Theo, I need to go somewhere, can you come with me?" I really thought for a few seconds about how I was going to propose him what I had in mind. I don't think he got the message through my eyes.

"Where? Everything is okay?"

He clearly didn't get the message and was enjoying himself. He noticed I was different, but he wasn't sure how.

"Can you meet me outside? I will leave first ... than you follow." I whispered in his ear, almost kissing it with my lips.

He nodded like a church boy.

While leaving, I stumbled into Benguela and Harlow under the stairs. They couldn't see me, but I saw them, and I heard them very well. I noticed Harlow had disappeared, but I had assumed she went to hand out food to the neediest and those most influenced to hate her.

"I don't have a good feeling about this," Benguela muttered

to Harlow.

"Me neither ... but what can we do." Harlow pressed her eyes trying to think of something.

"I think he let Gunda go for a reason ... he is going to ask something in return ... He always does." Benguela was referring to Mahamba. I could never understand their relationship. Was she a loyal servant to him or a loyal friend to Harlow? Harlow had shared with me that Benguela was the only one who never treated her less. There is always an angel amongst chaos.

"But what?"

"If something happens, I want you to know that you are special. You are chosen. Don't let anyone tell you otherwise," Benguela reassured her.

Benguela hugged Harlow, and her face appeared in the light shining from one of the rooms. She spotted me, so I rushed to the stairs, almost falling.

I wasn't sure what I witnessed, and I wasn't sure if I wanted to know the truth. Seeing that conversation had sobered me up, but I still had enough courage to do what I was about to do. Theo finally came, so I grabbed his hand and forced him to follow me. Vince would never allow me to pull him like that, like I owned him. Theo didn't ask questions; he just obeyed.

The forest was different from when I had arrived; like it was finally being treated right, just like me. I thought the rain had influenced it; something was more alive in it. On one of those warm days, Cunene had shared with Theo that years ago they had wanted to remove the mystical power from the trees because it was killing Caputo, but Mahamba had refused. He had wanted to control every thought. He didn't care about harming the forest, cutting the trees to make furniture to decorate their house, and make instruments for the leaders to entertain him with music.

I think that the cutting of trees retained the water and that's how the drought started. While the heavy rain became a destructive force because there weren't enough trees to retain the water. There was so much I had learned in the past months that I wanted to teach Mirror.

I entered the forest, walking backwards, facing Theo and inviting him with my eyes to do the same. He hesitated, trying to understand, but then followed my lead.

"Jodi ..."

There was something about the way he would say my name, it was like music. I wanted to keep hearing it.

"Theo." I hoped he felt the same when I said his.

"I love you, Jodi Collins." He walked towards me.

I was back being my true self, the one I was before I had been robbed of a normal life.

"I want to be with you."

He got closer, and held my chin, and kissed me like he wanted to swallow my lips whole.

"I have never stopped loving you," he continued. He kissed me so strongly that I felt my whole body being pushed to the ground. He only paused to profess his love. I didn't say anything just smiled. I didn't have to. Theo never expected anything from me, just me.

"I love you ... I thought I didn't, but I always have."

I tried to hold my head up; the position was not comfortable, but I tried my best to face him. I had my elbows on the grass, and I finally said something. I wasn't sure if I was influenced by the forest, or it was just the liquor. The thought that came to mind was whether Theo would accept Mirror as his own.

"I love Mirror."

It's like he read my mind. I wanted to say I loved Caleb, but the mystical power of the forest wasn't that strong on me. I had control of my words. I felt different but I knew it wasn't caused by the forest. I wanted to say everything to Theo, but I wasn't used to expressing myself like this. I don't think I ever told Vince I loved him. I wasn't allowed to talk about it because he considered it shallow and vulgar. According to him, we had bigger things ahead of us – fighting for peace.

I believed in the power of the forest because I had heard about forests like this, the Casamance, in another land, where there was mystical power in a secret root. In that land, they would hold fights in the forest, but they wouldn't be wounded. They could even cut themselves with sharp blades but would leave unharmed. This power was on one condition: they could never tell anyone about the forest. I guess they failed to protect the forest secret.

For me, Theo was sacred. With Vince, I could do it many times but because I didn't feel anything. With Theo, I could only do it once because I couldn't take more than that. He was so rough but at the same time so gentle, it felt like whatever he was doing to me was supposed to hurt, but I was numbed, and at the same time I could feel it. I thought about the different times in my life I had felt physical pain. When I was about to give birth to Mirror, Aunt Noli had wanted to take me to the hospital, but Vince didn't allow it; he was afraid they were going to do something to Mirror. Years later, Amina revealed that Vince had wanted me to feel pain; he wanted me to be strong. It was always a test with him; I always had to prove myself.

The pain I had felt having Mirror had made me want to die. The pleasure I felt every time I made love to Theo also made me want to die but a death that would represent that I have lived a happy life, that I reached the limit of happiness.

The next day, at Harlow's, we were finally seeing the fruits of the harvest.

"You look different." Harlow handed me a mug of warm tea. Harlow had taken the plants from the farms and boiled them. The tea smelled like peace and the so-called hope everyone bragged about it.

"Different?" I became red just like the Elikyan sand. Maybe they had heard us from Caputo.

"You have a new glow." Did she hear us? I tried to remember what had happened last night, but I couldn't think about it without smiling like a little girl.

"I guess Elikya is not so bad." I reciprocated the smile.

"I want to thank you guys for everything you have done for us."

"We didn't have a choice."

We both laughed. Adowa heard us and joined us. She shared that the Book was going door to door and people were intrigued by it. I remember going to Book studies against my will but then I began to crave being there. Part of the reason I joined this war was motivated by the Book. It felt like the words spoke to me and only me, I felt chosen by Them.

It wasn't only plants growing, we finally had tomatoes too. Mahamba was storing them to make a big soup for everyone. They call it the 'solidarity soup'. Harlow said that they usually do it once a year to show how generous they are, but she saw it as a distraction. I wondered what they were hiding this year. I didn't care to be honest; I was too focused on going home and starting a life with Theo. I also didn't care about Mariane. Ever since I turned sixteen I had been concerned about everyone else. It was time to be selfish! I wanted to get married. I always had since I was young; that was my purpose in life, my shallow purpose. Is it really that bad to just want a normal life, with a husband and kids? That's the thing about Theo; he allowed me to be myself. I don't think it ever crossed Vince's mind; he would probably say that people like him were robbed of a fairytale because of the whites. Sometimes I feel like he enjoyed his emotional misery. You know what else bothered me? The fact that he had never called me beautiful. When I finally gathered the courage to ask him, with the chance of being completely humiliated, or to find some glimpse of his feelings, he said he didn't want me to be a vain woman. He reinforced that I had bigger things ahead of me than to worry about beauty.

What about Mirror? What about how the black side would react? I wanted to stop caring but I just couldn't. Mirror loved his father, even though he was only months old when Vince passed. He would beg me to tell him stories about the amazing Vince. Vince was indeed amazing, an amazing father, but I don't think he was a good lover. I wish he had more time to show how good of a father he was. I didn't have doubts about that, I could tell just from the way he looked at Mirror. Vince was someone who grew up without love; it took him a lot of work to be a good father. I remember when Mirror was born, the first time he saw him, he smiled; Vince never smiled. He smiled like a little kid, like plants growing in drought, like people dancing in the rain … I held onto those littles moments to survive. I couldn't be a mother alone, it was too hard, I didn't have in me. I wasn't just a mother; I was the mother of the first mixed child in Rhodesia allowed to live. I wasn't just a mother; I was the mother of a black boy with *thriller* ... I wasn't just a mother; I was the mother of the symbol of peace ... Tears fell down my eyes thinking about those times. No matter how dark my thoughts were, the image of Vince holding his son was the light, it kept me going. Otherwise I would end up just like my mother. But then again, I was the black sheep of my family; I couldn't follow her footsteps. Giving up was not an option, when I had been able to make a man like Vince smile.

I remember him explaining to me that Mirror meant that our son wasn't black or white, he was whatever he saw in a Mirror, so we would make sure he saw greatness. While I was pregnant, he mentioned other names, like Marley. It was the name of a singer and activist who fought for peace in his land, he preached unity and was able to make leaders from opposing political groups sit down to have peaceful conversations. I remember Vince sitting at his desk telling me all those stories of men who fought for something bigger than them. There was Martin. He was from a land ruled by whites, and he fought for the black's rights, he was religious and preached about a nonviolent war and later was killed. And there was Raúl, just a simple guy, who wanted a family and one day the military shot him in the neck.

I could never understand people who were tortured for fighting for peace. Vince only told me about their accomplishments. Aunt Noli was the one who told me about how they were killed, with the hope of making me stop what I was doing. I didn't want my son to inherit these people's struggles, so when he said the name Mirror, I accepted it instantly. It didn't matter what name Mirror had, the black side were going to nickname whatever they wanted; they didn't care about white baptism and registered white names.

"Always in your head, Jodi."

Gunda joined me after the two inseparable women, Adowa and Harlow, left. They were probably getting the Book to pass it on to the next house.

"Yes, that's me ... How you holding up?"

"I am okay. I like this land, there's something about it." He looked around. He was still getting to know everyone.

"Hunger."

I gave him naughty smile.

"Well ... They don't look bothered by it ... They seem to be okay ... We can't fight for people who are not aware they are being oppressed." His voice was soft and rusty which made what he said sound wise.

"I am learning that ... and accepting that." I realized that everyone was tired of fighting.

"You look different, Jodi." He sounded just like Harlow earlier. His words carried the same meaning but coming from Gunda they felt deeper because he had known me longer.

"Aha. Well, I am almost forty."

"You know I am not talking about that ... hummm." He wasn't sure how to say what he was going to say. His sweat made his cacao skin shine.

"I know."

I gave him a discreet smile because I wasn't sure how he felt about me and Theo, but I knew he was talking about him. Theo indeed made me lighter; I had always been angry after being with Vince.

"Vince could never love you the way you deserve."

He chose not to face me, but I didn't have to look into his eyes to know how truthful his statement was.

"Hmm ... Vince ... was..."

I couldn't say anything. I knew he didn't meant in a bad way, but I felt the need to defend the father of my son.

"Juvey was right about you." Gunda didn't stop showering me with compliments.

"Gunda I don't want to talk about her ... not today." I was having a good day; I didn't want to talk about the past. Even though the past lived in my mind, I avoided mentioning it. In my mind, I could hate myself, but not out loud. I didn't want anyone to know that I regretted everything, and I hated myself for not saving my sister.

"I had a dream about her ... I need to tell you this ... Because she told me to tell you ... I was in prison when I dreamt about her ... She was okay ... She was holding a baby in her arms and she told me that you showed people that love exist, and that you have big things ahead of you." He wasn't holding back. It was strange because he always kept to himself, he never wanted to talk, just like the black elders. It was like they would pretend things never happened. I could never understand that, maybe I wasn't traumatized enough to sympathize with their coping mechanism.

"Me? I don't want to do this anymore." I started sobbing. The words were not coming how they were supposed to, but he understood. I was finally retiring from this life of fighting and hearing that my sister still thought I had it in me was calling me back to be this person I wanted to move on from.

"Jodi ... she just wants you to live your life and be happy ... She also wants you to know that she is happy."

My whole body cried; my back curved trying to keep me together. He stood up and held my head. I could hear his stomach and smell him; he smelled like dark plants. I couldn't stop crying. My sister was my breaking point. My whole life, I had looked up to her; I mimicked her in everything. I wasn't the one who stood in front of the Rhodesians and recited crimes; it was Juvey. I wasn't the one who had a mixed child, it was Juvey. I was whatever she wanted me to be. What love was he talking about? I don't think I loved Vince. Or the love for my son? I almost didn't have Mirror...

I didn't need Gunda's blessing to be with Theo, especially now that I was so unapologetic in my decisions, but I had always felt like I owed him, and this conversation set me free. I was so upset that I was basically chewing his shirt, so I pulled my face away. My eyes were reddish, and my eyelashes stuck together. I tried cleaning the tears before someone came.

We heard a lot of out of noise coming from the main alley. Adowa and Harlow came and explained that people were fighting in the queues for the solidarity soup and complaining that some of them were getting more than others. I stood up to try to glance to the scene. I could see a big pan with people surrounding it, while Luanda was trying to calm them down. The other leaders came to rescue him. I saw Moxico climb onto the table to try to calm the crowd, but they were furious. I could see the steam from the pan, and smell the savory liquid in which meat, fish, and vegetables simmered. That soup made my stomach feel peaceful just thinking about it. My body, and probably Gunda's too, longed for it. The whole land was filled with the smell of the spices and meat, or at least animals' bones. The people who already had been served, sat on the floor, chewing the bones. I wanted to join them, but the queues were all the way to the entrance of Elikya. People were pushing each other and trying to remove people who they deemed undeserving.

I thought I heard someone in the queue reciting the Book.

I wasn't certain if I heard correctly but seeing Harlow's and Adowa's reactions. I could tell I was right.

"Then THEY declared – I am the bread of life. Whoever comes to me will never go hungry, and whoever believes in me will never be thirsty."

We decided to get closer. Should we be proud of our work or fear for our lives? I looked up to see if Mahamba was on the roof, but he was nowhere to be found. Luanda was busy trying to calm them down, while Moxico started to be more aggressive when his strategy of standing on the table didn't work. I stepped in front of a woman he threatened to hit. My face was 3 centimeters away from his; I could smell his gravy breath. The women looked white, but she wasn't, her facial hair was a weird blond, and her hair was dry, not silky like mine. There were only a few white people in this village, but she was different. she appeared like a black person dipped in white skin. I could tell her eyesight was weak, because she kept squinting to see who I was. She pushed me away from the queue, thinking I was trying to get ahead of her. I almost fell on the floor. Theo ran towards me and caught me before I fell. Adowa was in line trying to hear more and see who knew about the Book. They tried to recognize the people they lent the Book, but there were so many at this point, they couldn't remember.

"Leave! You came here to laugh at us!!" shouted a woman with a familiar face.

"Calm down." Theo tried to stop the woman from hitting Harlow.

I recognized that face, it was the gypsy woman Harlow had given food to a few months before. Her hair was black – darker than anything, almost blue, silky and strong; like you could use it to make clothes or a blanket. I only noticed Harlow when I followed the woman's eyes. I didn't know who she was referring to. Harlow was just standing there, not moving. Sometimes we become so afraid of upsetting people that we silence ourselves to not rub people the wrong way. While Harlow froze, there was so much anger in the woman's eyes, like Harlow was the reason for their hunger.

"What is your problem? Are you mad? This woman has been nothing but good to you and your family." I intervened.

I just couldn't let her treat my dear friend like that. I remembered Harlow giving the woman a bigger portion of food than the others, because she had kids, and now the woman was fighting with her people because of quantities of food. Does hunger make you lose morals and principles?

"She is too full of herself!" She almost spit on Harlow. And poor Harlow didn't move, like she felt deserved that, but I knew very well she didn't. There was nothing that these people could say to me for me to change my opinion of her.

I held Harlow's hand, and I took her from there. Theo accompanied us, and Adowa stayed behind. I was glad we left because I couldn't bear their smell. At every step of the queue I inhaled another sweaty, savory scent. The people smelled like spoiled soup. As I breathed their smells, the air became contaminated. I remembered Aunt Noli telling me that I smelled different after spending time in the black side. I couldn't notice what she meant, but I remember the smell my aunt described was the same one I noticed when I first started hanging around with them. It wasn't bad, it was just different; like sweat became permanent in the body. She also said I spoke differently, like my tongue was imitating their tongues. Knowing my aunt, she didn't mean any harm with the comments, she just meant that I was becoming theirs.

'She is too full of herself'. I kept thinking about that. That's all! Nothing else. They hated Harlow because she was too full of herself. Whenever you hear someone talking ill of someone else and you ask them why they don't like the person in question, if the answer is something like 'I don't like the way she walks', or something so vain, bear in mind that it is jealousy in the flesh. If you can't back up your feeling with an evidence of an issue, it's pure hatred.

That night, I could hear Adowa struggling to sleep and moving her body. It must hurt to have nightmares on the floor. I wanted to be awake in case she woke up disturbed, but I fell asleep. But it wasn't for long. In my sleep, I knew she was going to wake me up with some disturbing news. I wanted her to finish the dream and then deliver the information. I didn't wish those kinds of dreams on anyone, but we needed to be alerted to protect ourselves.

"No ... No ... No ... No."

She was fighting with the sheets, moving them from side to side, like she was cleaning the floor.

"Enough!"

I knew it was time to wake her up, she couldn't take it anymore. When I had those dreams, I wanted them to last so I could figure out the whole picture but sometimes the pain of an unfortunate future was unbearable.

"We need to save her."

I could see her breathing trying to slow down and keep the same pace as her heart. I was relieved that she didn't say 'him', so it meant that Theo and Mirror were saved. But then I started thinking about Harlow; I hoped nothing would happen to her.

"Who? Who, Adowa?" I tried to hold her and calm her down.

"She doesn't deserve this." She was shaking.

"Adowa, calm down!"

"We've got to do something about it." She composed herself and was ready to resume her sleeping like nothing happened.

"We will." I knew I couldn't ask more questions. Having those dreams askes for a certain grace to keep a secret. I struggled when I was young. I had dreams that were encrypted messages telling me that Juvey was going to die, but still I didn't know what to do.

"I need to tell you something ... when I was in prison, I dreamt about Mirror ... It wasn't just him ... Nicola was there too and Theo's son and a black man. But they were all okay." She didn't give me time to react, turned her back and slept.

"A black man," I repeated. I wanted to ask more, but I knew Adowa couldn't take anymore. When sharing these dreams there are consequences. Even though she had told me they were okay, every dream means something. I don't remember Caleb ever hanging out with Mirror with Nicola. And a black man? Who?

I slept with all those thoughts trying to provoke a dream, maybe I could dream the same dream and it would last longer so I could find out the end.

Chapter 8

I held Harlow's hand. She didn't seem like herself; I had never seen her in such a state since we arrived. Whenever we go through something, there is always one person who helps us and is there for us. For Harlow, that person was Benguela. Benguela had a motherly love for Harlow and if Harlow survived all of the injustice and unfair judgements in this town, it was thanks to her. A light rain started to fall and not everyone noticed straight away; the drops were absorbed by the thick layers of our garments. We were all wearing traditional prints that belonged to Benguela's tribes. The rain was purifying us and reminding us that the nature is our true leader.

Benguela's tribe had prepared everything; they didn't ask Mahamba for anything. They made sure that the little they had would be used for the funeral. They buried Benguela quietly, in the yard of her own house, and not a lot of people came. Present were the incredible five, Mahamba and the leaders, and her people. It was tradition of her people to bury deceased bodies in the grounds of their own houses. People from other tribes were usually buried beyond their houses, in land beside the farms. Harlow once told me that she believed that the drought was a result of burying wicked souls next to the plantation.

The soft rain poured onto Benguela's coffin; the hissing sound felt like a blessing from her. We knew that she was at peace and watching over us, especially Harlow. I kept holding Harlow to check her heartbeats. She released my hand, and I could see she wasn't really present. I wanted to join her in her thoughts and tell her that whatever she was feeling, it was going to pass. I tried to concentrate on the eulogies, but the speakers were talking in their own dialects. I had heard them before, but I still couldn't understand the words. The speakers made clicking sounds by placing the tips of their tongues on the roofs of their mouths, near their incisors. For years, the black side tried to teach me how to do it, but I couldn't. My excuse was that my tongue was too short.

After her family finished speaking, they asked Adowa to sing. When they had come to deliver the news, they had invited Adowa to offer her condolences through singing. Harlow had explained that this was an uncommon request, since this tribe didn't usually sing at their burials, but I guess they wanted to do something special for Benguela.

"JEZU NGO, MUENE UA TUITIA ... U TUENDESA UM MUENHU IÚ ... KANA-KU DINGI DIKAMBA DIENGI ... INGANA JEZU, MUENE KAMBA DIETU ... JEZU NGÓ, JEZU NGÓ ... LATUSAKE MIXIMA IETU ... JEZU NGÓ, JEZU NGO."

Adowa was giving her best vocals to honor Benguela. This song was traumatic for me; they sang it at Vince's funeral and at every funeral on the black side. I had wanted to stop attending funerals, but they said it would not look good for me. That's when I realized the blacks were very traditional, and always put a front.

The birds flew away, trying to get away from this sadness.

They always looked like they knew what they were doing; they were not clueless like the other animals. Though the other animals didn't have wings to run away like the birds. Speaking of animals, they killed one in her honor. I wasn't not sure what animal it was, but I knew they were going to eat it later. I wondered why they wanted to farm if their diet was so carnivorous.

I wanted my mind to take me away from there, but my mind wasn't a safe place. I had finally realized that all those years I had spent saying that Adowa wasn't okay was an act, so that I could look okay. Adowa expressed her feelings; I didn't. People often do that; they try to frame someone for a crime they are committing. I tried to concentrate on my hands, particular my nails. I started playing with my cuticles. They hurt whenever I touched them, but I wanted to feel pain so I would stop thinking. Playing with my skin, moving the thin layers, was like the feeling of stirring my memories till I found something that completely destroyed me.

I looked over to Benguela's people. They all looked the same: dirty water tone with soft white features. The kids, struggling to make sense of this, all had shaved heads. It was part of their acts of mourning. Theo had heard that they all came from the same man; that years ago, a single man was used to procreate and make a lot of children. It is believed that he was the father of more 3000 people. It made me think about something I had heard my dad, and some other lawyers, talking about. That in a modern and advanced land people were placing specially prepared white men's sperm directly in the uterus of white women, to make sure the new generation was all white. I think that the past and the future at some point they meet.

They lowered her light-brown, wooden coffin into a hole. I

144

saw the veins of the pallbearers stand out which showed how heavy the coffin was. They covered the coffin with dark brown sand. The color was unique: completely different from the red sand around the village and the peanut brown of the farms. There was a small window at the top of the coffin that allowed us to see Benguela. Her umber tone was pale and there was no color in her face, except her eyes: they were a bit red. Maybe it was some kind of weird practice they had in her tribe to redden the eyes of the deceased. Adowa's voice was slowly dying, as they covered the coffin with sand. People started to leave. Some were crying, others were arguing about who gave the most contribution to her burial, and others were mourning in silence.

I walked out with Theo and Gunda, accompanying the people. We were supposed to walk around the whole town, but I used the opportunity to sneak away to the leaders' house. I left unannounced. The blacks had taught me that people don't say bye at funerals or at burial gatherings. I wondered who had created all these rules. Someone had just woken up and decided on these whole procedures and itineraries to follow.

Benguela's passing was the last straw; I was ready to go home. I needed to talk Mahamba, in private, no leaders, no musketeers, just us. He had left the funeral early. He had seemed to not be taking this well because he kept rubbing his eyes like crazy.

I wanted to prepare very well what I was going to say. Going against one person with very firm beliefs was a suicide mission. People like him started with good intentions, they wanted to protect their people, but along the way greed and power got into them. Mahamba was a brilliant mind and natural leader; he had been able to influence the whole town to believe that hunger was holy. He had created a culture of obedience and gratitude, through manipulation and starvation.

When I arrived, the house was silent; everyone was part of the vigil march. I noticed that the heavy rains had also affected the house, not a lot, but it wasn't the same. It looked worn, especially with so many people staying there. I could never finish counting the rooms: every time I came, I found a new area. Harlow had told us that it used to be a center to train people with skills like tailoring, pottery, soap-making and the likes. I entered each division, silently, checking who was around. No one. I checked each room, they were all filled with boxes of objects, probably used for the trainings. When Theo was staying here, he overhead that most of things the people made were for the leaders to wear or use, like cutlery, clothes, and the likes. There was dust in every step of the stairs, and I couldn't help but sneeze.

"Who is there? Cabinda?" Mahamba enquired. He sounded alarmed, like I had caught him doing something bad.

"It's me, Jodi."

"Oh Jodi, come in please." He pretended that it was something completely normal for me to just show up at his place. I entered and looked around his office, at the shelves with many books, all covered with dust. He was sitting behind a wooden desk loaded with more books and handmade things. I guessed that these were probably gifts to express gratitude for all of his generous favors.

"I keep them here, for safety. You know I don't want people stealing for me," he said, following my every move. His tone was sarcastic, and it implied he knew Benguela stole the books.

"Why would they steal if they could just come and borrow one? You wouldn't mind, right? Otherwise, why are you keeping them?"

I grabbed one and wiped off the dust. I was finally learning

146

how to deal with these people – playing the game. Mahamba wasn't violent; he reminded me of my people. The blacks were loud, they liked the show. If they were going to do something to you, it would be out loud, in the open, while the whites played with your head. But here, there was no war between black or white.

"Well Jodi, I am just protecting them. One day you will understand." He shook his head.

"Are you?" I stared at him, and noticed how crumpled his face was, like he just woke up or he wasn't feeling well. I observed his eyes; the corneas looked different. I moved closer, and he made a gesture for me to sit.

"Why aren't you there with others? I know Benguela was a great friend to you."

"Yes, she was. She was a dear friend. Her absence will be felt." I was nonchalant, just like him.

"I am glad you came. I wanted to talk to you guys about something, but I didn't want to be insensitive after Benguela's passing."

Insensitive? A great choice of word, I thought. He had this soft voice that was annoying, it was like if you had to show people how evil he was, no one would believe it because of his tone.

"I see. I also have something to tell you. Let us go! We have done everything you have asked!"

"I am afraid I can't do that."

He leaned back in the chair, sitting more carefully.

"Mahamba ... I have a family back home ... I can't live here forever ... Let's have Gunda's Babemba tomorrow ... What are we waiting for?"

I made a mockery of this land with my tone. I don't know how, but it came out like that.

147

"I can't just wake up and host a Babemba."

"Yes, you can!"

I made another condescending facial expression, emphasizing that I thought this system was lame.

"You don't understand. People are different now. There are many Babembas already planned, and we need to give them priority."

"You don't care about these people. You do whatever pleases you. Whatever Mahamba wants."

"You don't know me, Jodi. Everything I have done in this land is because of the people." He kept moving his chair, showing how uncomfortable this conversation was making him.

"Starving them?? Making them illiterate? For their own good." I pressed my eyes, and I probed him.

"You don't know what you are talking about!" His tone made me feel naïve, it sounded like there was more to his ideologies.

"You decide how much people will eat. You know that what you give them it's not enough!"

I was getting emotional, and my tone showed how much.

"People will never be satisfied. They kill each other because of food. Food makes them greedy. I can't take food from them ... but I can keep them in check. They need to have the same quantities. No one can be better than anyone else. A child shouldn't feel superior to another child because in their home they have more food. I can't let that happen!" He spoke more loudly, but he wasn't screaming. The image of the people in the solidarity food distribution fighting each other came into my mind.

I chose my words carefully; I can't lie that his argument challenged me, but I remained firm.

"It's not the things that divide us – it's our internal problems.

A child doesn't hate himself because he is poor, but because he can't find gratitude in the little that he has."

"Gratitude. Gratitude. It's hard to be grateful you know. Some people can't. You don't know what you are talking about. I have given my life for these people." He started wiping the dust from the table. I followed him with my eyes; I could tell his nose was stuffy or runny, and his eyes became red and watery. Was he trying to hide tears?

"I know you believe that." I almost laughed.

"Not everything is what it looks like."

"Tell me something that I am not seeing. I only see hunger and ignorance."

"I have created a land free from prejudice, segregation, hate. My people are free to do whatever they want."

He smiled discreetly, a smile he couldn't quite hide.

"What is freedom without food?" I turned around to face him. "Jodi."

"If they were free, they would speak up for others at the Babembas. They would say something but after all these years of mental oppression they lack so much confidence." I wanted to see the reaction to every word I spoke in his face.

"Don't believe everything you hear. I am not a monster!" He put the books back and went back to his seat.

"I wish you were. Monsters show their true colors through their features. Others pretend." I stood up and I was ready to go.

"Sit … I told you I had something to talk to you about."

"I am listening." I remained standing.

"There still something else I need you guys to plant." I knew exactly what he was talking about.

"I see … We do this and Gunda's Babemba is scheduled

149

immediately." I had learned this trick with Theo. I wasn't a good negotiator, but I tried.

"Fair enough." He nodded.

I started walking towards the door. He stopped me.

"Jodi ... ask your friend why she never spoke up for anyone in one of the Babembas." He was referring to Harlow. He knew Harlow was feeding me all this bravery. They were a bit similar to be honest, but they just lived in parallel universes of thinking. People like that apply strong convictions to their lives to protect them from something. Being a child abandoned in this lost town, I could see what Harlow was protecting herself from but what was Mahamba protecting himself from?

People join religion and follow firm beliefs to have a purpose in life. It's as though they need to believe in something outrageous to feel like they are different, holy, or better than others. They create those ideologies to send the message that they are in control. That they are stubborn and not willing to be flexible or to accept others thinking in any context. In some cases it is for the sake of being tough. In others, they are bored, and they find pleasure in it. They create their own shells to protect themselves from the world, and to keep others out.

I stopped for a few seconds, but I don't think he wanted an answer. When I reached the stairs, I recognized another smell. It smelled like roasted onions or the sweat from saggy boobs. Namibe showed up, sweating from carrying the coffin. He mumbled that we needed to talk, and we agreed to meet.

When I returned to Harlow's, I could hear the arguing from outside. Gunda was the loudest and Theo followed, and then Adowa and Harlow. I opened the door carefully and they all looked at me, Theo wondered with his eyes where I had been, while Gunda continued his argument.

"They used to hunt animals for meat and came in contact with their infected blood."

"No, Harlow said that Benguela came here because she was completely mistreated in her land," Adowa intervened.

Both Gunda and Adowa were levelheaded. Harlow was silent but she looked at me, like she knew I had just been fed some kind of lie about her. People can tell when you start looking at them differently.

"Yes, I heard it came from a land with predominately black people," Theo added.

"You mean that it was purposely spread in a land to kill black people." Gunda instantly became aggressive.

"In one of the houses we used to go teach, a woman shared with me that Benguela was known for being a promiscuous woman and that she contracted the illness from being intimate with different men in her land – white or black – that is not the issue," Adowa asserted. She had good intentions with her argument, but it triggered Harlow, I could see the blood coming up to her face.

"Benguela wasn't promiscuous. You guys don't know what you are talking about. She lived her whole life fighting it. She tried herbs, different plants but she would always fall sick. She read so much about it, trying to find a cure but..." She didn't reveal how she had contracted the illness; she still owned her friend confidentiality.

The whole room was silent.

"Harlow we didn't mean any harm ... we just want to help." Gunda touched her hand.

"I know." She held his hand and immediately let it go, like

she was afraid of intimacy. She was ready to go to her room and properly mourn but I stopped her.

"I need to talk to you guys." I focused my gaze on Theo and Gunda because they were the ones who could fix this. Theo wanted to ask me where I had been, but he knew he couldn't be that obvious in front of people.

"Mahamba still wants us to do something for him. To plant something," I said, afraid of their reactions.

"Dark plants." Harlow guessed it, she already had Mahamba all figured out; she knew his every move.

"You know dark plants?" Adowa looked at Harlow surprised.

"We had them in my land. I don't remember what they look like. But Benguela warned me that Mahamba wouldn't let you guys go ... that he wanted something from you guys," Harlow revealed.

"He wants us to start soon. He knows we have the seeds," I divulged.

"How did he know? It feels like he is always a step ahead," Adowa asked, hysterically.

"He knows everything," Harlow said.

"So, we plant them and then what?" Gunda replied. I could see he was okay with giving up the seeds, since this was his life we were taking about.

"Your Babemba will take place and they will decide your fate," I muttered, afraid that I might had done a bad deal.

"Why is his Babemba taking so long?" Theo asked.

My insecurities told me he was tired of this land and wanted to go home to Caleb, and his wife. Gunda's fate would also decide the fate of me and Theo.

"There are so many happening now. They don't invite us because they are afraid of what we might do there, but I hear the

152

people walking there every other week. Benguela told me that Gunda's Babemba was going to be delayed," Harlow said.

I could tell that there was something she was holding back. When she said 'Benguela' it seemed as she had something in her throat, and she couldn't swallow it.

"Why? What's happening?" Theo pleaded. Theo didn't do well with suspense and half-truths.

"I think I know. When I went to the prison to get the Book, the inmates looked different. They were reading the Book. They were talking about it, discussing it. There was something there," Adowa said.

"Yes. All they talked about it was the Book. I remember. They used to read to each other and some were teaching others to read with the Book. I would fall asleep listening to the verses – that's what kept me going." Gunda joined Adowa in their shared memories of the prison.

"So, they understand their rights now? And they want to fight for them," Theo summarized, without any emotional tone. "We wanted this, right? That was the plan." Theo reminded us.

We wanted to help them but not to get in the way of our own plans and our mission to go back home. In that moment, I didn't care about Babembas and people fighting for their freedom, I cared about my freedom, and seeing my son. I thought about Mahamba; maybe he wasn't a monster.

The mood shifted; I think we all realized we were hypocrites. Harlow went to her room; I could hear her crying. Theo and Gunda continued to discuss Benguela's disease. I didn't want to talk about these things anymore, why would nature try to kill us? I was tired of finding out more disturbing things about this life. I was developing wounds in my scalp from always scratching, I was tired of thinking and trying to find solutions to everlasting

153

problems. We could never win. Our own body could betray us?! I knew we were not safe inside of our minds but at least our body should be strong enough to protect us.

In our room, Adowa resorted to singing but in a very low tone, so quiet, like an acapella, so it wouldn't disturb me, instead it would help me fall asleep. She switched between singing and laughing. She would do that from time to time. She once explained that she would think about something funny, and she would laugh. I always wanted to tell her that I had the same urge, but I controlled it. It's like you live in your head so much that you become your best company. Back on the black side, I felt so alone, and I didn't know who I could share my thoughts with, so I kept to myself. Sometimes my thoughts would burst into laughs, but very low ones; I didn't want to be deemed crazy. It was enough to be considered insane by your own people, so at least I wanted to be praised by the blacks.

We waited for Mahamba and his beehives next to the sacred tree. They all came this time, except Benguela. The weird thing about a death is that on the day you receive the news you think everything is going to stop and that life will be completely different from that day on but then a few days pass and nothing has changed; it is like the person never existed. Seeing the people from afar, I had the impression that I was watching a cult. They were wearing their long attire that never looked appropriate for any event: they must have suffocated in those garments. I wondered what their legs looked like. They were probably pale from being deprived of any sun.

"Jodi, Adowa, Theo, Gunda ... Once again thanks for helping our land." Mahamba glanced at each of us.

"We are here to serve, sir." Adowa bowed in a sarcastic way.

"We all came to wish you a pleasant cultivation. I think the sacred tree is the perfect place. It will wish you fruitful plantation and watch over you. This is a sacred place." He ignored Adowa. I don't think he was really fond of her; he found her annoying.

"Let's start ... We don't have time to waste!" Theo looked to Gunda to give him a sign to hand over the seeds. I never found out where they hid the seeds, and I didn't care to ask.

"Wait ... Cabinda, Bengo, Luanda and Moxico will be here to assist you with anything you need." Mahamba smiled looking at each of us.

"Assist?!" Gunda's expression showed his disapproval. The blacks had never shared the dark plants recipe with anyone, not even me, after almost twenty years of living with them. It was supposed to be Adowa and Gunda planting and me and Theo watching – or running away to make love.

"We won't be any trouble, we promise." Cabinda held both his hands together, lacing his fingers.

"I see. In that case, we would like Harlow to join us please." Adowa stepped in front of Mahamba. He nodded and the leaders looked at each other.

Gunda turned his back and started the process. He didn't have time for drama and useless arguments. He started digging. Theo and the leaders followed. They brought Harlow like she was a prisoner. I wasn't sure why Adowa wanted her there considering they were so careful with the plants. I guess she wanted to have something to negotiate with, or, perhaps, to make Harlow feel included. She wasn't coping well with Benguela's passing and it showed. She rarely left her room or talked to us. They dropped Harlow to her knees and ordered her to start planting.

155

"Tell me about the weather of this land." Gunda ordered Luanda, while continuing to sow. He was fast and agile.

"It is very dry and hot. We went through long periods of drought. Then it rained so much. I don't know. What do you need to know?"

I realized that Gunda had spent most of his time here in jail. I imagined how difficult it must have been for him to not see the sun for months. He had some kind of mystical relation with the sun and nature itself. He had taught us that the seeds had high germination and that they could tell we were in trouble. I have seen people speaking to themselves, and even animals, but to seeds? Wow!

"Is it ever humid?"

Gunda looked around trying to smell the weather. I wasn't sure what he wanted but Vince always told me that dark plants were tolerant to high humidity.

"I don't think so." Luanda wanted to help but he wasn't sure what Gunda wanted.

"We need to finish sowing today." Gunda shouted.

I sat on the roots of the sacred tree. The branches coming from the base gave us a support to lean on. Harlow lay next to me; I think she needed a shoulder to cry on, but she wouldn't dare cry in front of the leaders. Adowa was laying on the ground reciting something that sounded like another language. I recognized them as abundance declarations. We heard her say, "'Sat, Chit, Ananda ... Tat Tvam Asi ... Om Vardhanam Namah ... Om Ritam Namah ... Om Daksham Namah ... Om Varunam Namah'." Since she had left prison, she had told me that she wanted to make sure her life was worthy; that her life wasn't in vain. She had declared that she wanted to live an abundant life and that everything that she wanted was in the earth. Every morning, I heard her repeat,

156

'existence, consciousness, bliss ... I nourish the universe and the universe nourishes me ... My life is in harmony ... I am divine'. It was refreshing to wake up with positivity.

"How are you holding up?"

I realized it was the perfect moment to talk Harlow. We had never been left alone since the fantastic three had joined us. I wasn't sure what I wanted from her, but my conversation with Mahamba had made me see her in a different light.

"I am okay. I knew one day this was going to happen," she said with a calm tone.

People who go through trauma they think they shouldn't be traumatized by anything anymore; they force themselves to take everything normally.

"Grief makes you look at life in a different way."

I was trying to see how I was going to dump what I wanted to say.

"Where were you the other day? After the funeral."

She knew something was off. I think the worst thing you can do to someone who helped you is question their character.

"Hum ... I went to see Mahamba." I hesitated. I hunched my back against the tree; I was starting to develop the only curve in my body.

"I know," she said, confidently.

"Is it possible that he is not the monster that we think he is?" I was conflicted.

"He got into your head, huh?"

"I don't know. He said a lot of things. It makes me question." I gazed at her, at her patches, and her whole being.

"It's okay, Jodi. You don't need to believe me. You have done enough for me." She knew what I was implying, it felt like I had questioned her whole story.

157

"Harlow ... why all this animosity towards you? What have you done?" I straightened myself to sit and face her. She was still lying down, unbothered.

"Hmm ... you know people want victims to be perfect. I never said I was perfect."

"Why do they treat you like that?"

"I used to ask myself the same question until it made me hate myself. People like to be offended – they enjoy having someone on whom they can dispose all of their anger. They don't care if you are this person they created in their head. They just don't. They are hungry for retribution. It´s convenient for them. They pick the sides that give them the best benefit ... They are weak." She didn't look bothered by my suspicion. She was proud of who she was, and I guess that confidence was what annoyed them even more.

"But why you?"

"If you see a light in the tunnel would you ask how it got there, or you would just run towards it? People want an escape from their problems ... Someone who they can dispose all of their hate and anger. Upon." She sounded like a calmer version of the insane Adowa. How did she know all these things? I asked myself. I guess when you don't have anyone, your wisdom becomes your protection. The fact that she had figured everything out; that's what had made her even more hated.

"But you don't deserve this." It was the least I could say after questioning her. I had begun this conversation with good intentions, but they had been derailed.

"My mother used to say that people instantly join forces to do good." She gave me a look that I translated as 'do I deserve you questioning me'. I wanted to shut up.

"Your mother was a good woman. She is probably proud of

you." I tried to save my soul.

"She was wrong ... It's easier for people to join forces to do evil." She scratched her ear, like she had an infection.

I was silent. I always wondered what it meant when people were silent during a conversation, now I knew; it was shame.

Moxico approached us. I wasn't sure if he wanted to rest, or if he was trying to listen to the conversation. I was glad he came so that I didn't feel so bad for questioning my friend. Why is it that whenever people need us the most, we fail them?

"We really need this — it will save a lot of people."

"They also need food and education."

I looked to Harlow, trying to apologize to her. She was in her thoughts, probably suffering, and apparently admiring her long feet. Aunt Noli said that if a woman has a long feet, it means she was supposed to be taller and maybe they would respect her more.

"Don't listen to ungrateful people." It was a dig at Harlow. He grabbed one of the lowest branches.

"Who should I listen to then?" I probed him.

"The plants could have saved Benguela."

When he said 'Benguela', I could feel Harlow's body temperature changing. She leaned on the tree, then she stood and left.

"Where are you going?" Cabinda appeared and shouted at her.

She continued to walk. They all wanted a piece of her, but she couldn't be controlled, and when people can't control you, they label you problematic.

"What's happening there?" I asked Cabinda, as I spotted people moving in the direction of Caputo. It was loud: they were carrying drums and slamming them until their hands hurt.

"There's a Babemba today."

The people around looked different, like they finally had the guts and strength to stand up for themselves and each other.

"Don't you need to be there? I thought all the leaders should be at the Babemba, to make sure the decision was fair."

"Mahamba will make sure his fate is fair," he replied, and left me there.

I guess stealing our dark plants recipe was more important than deciding's someone fate.

We couldn't ignore the noise, but we also didn't care enough to go there and participate. I saw a man being persecuted. I wondered if Gunda had met him in prison. I heard Cabinda and Luanda talking about his story and saying that he had killed a woman many years ago. I wondered if they cared what kind of person he was, and if he had committed the crime he was accused of. I think men have a pass for everything; men were allowed to be angry and upset. When a man talks in a rude tone, he is considered upset in that moment. When a woman increases her voice, she is bossy. Men are not labelled and given an adjective. Vince used to say that the world wasn't kind to beautiful women. I think the world wasn't kind to any women. Was this man not given a Babemba before because he was too ignorant to ask, or because they never felt like the woman deserved justice? Why men hated women so much? I got angry when I thought about how many years of abuse women endured.

Chapter 9

A few days passed and we patiently waited for the plants to blossom. Mahamba called us again and told us to meet at the sacred tree. The leaders looked disappointed as they waited for us, their hands in fists. As we approached, I saw Mahamba crouching down, touching the plants that didn't look so good.

"They are dead!" Cabinda shouted.

"Wait, calm down ... There must be an explanation."

Their reactions seemed ominous.

"There is an explanation," Adowa said. "Dark plants are about intentions. Whatever intention your pour into making them is what will come out ... ´what you reap, you must sow´ ... Om Ritam Namah'. My intentions and desires are supported by the cosmos," Adowa explained this in her Zen voice. She then quoted something else, but no one knew what it meant, and no one dared to ask questions. They were so desperate for the plants that they were going to do whatever we wanted.

Mahamba was silently admiring how the herb grew and its stem fell.

Gunda was doing the same, he knew dark plants very well.

Armel had taught him how to plant them and take care of them.

"You gave us the wrong seeds!!!" Cabinda pulled Gunda's shirt and accused him.

Gunda didn't retaliate, because he knew the power of his anger and how final it was.

"No. We gave you the right seeds, we taught you how to do it, but you planted them. It was between you and them."

Adowa separated them.

I was with Theo the whole time; we didn't want to interfere because we didn't know much about the plants.

"We need the plants; a lot of things could be avoided if we had the plants," Mahamba said.

I had to say something. "Don't blame the plants on how you choose to govern your people. You don't understand what the plants are for. They have saved people. They have also killed them."

The leaders looked at each other, choked.

Juvey came to my mind and Theo held my hands tighter because he knew what the reverse intention of the plants did to my family.

"Killed?" Bengo asked.

I had almost forgotten about him. I hated that about me, not being able to memorize names and people, it made me arrogant by default.

"Listen, we want to help you, but you need to promise us that you will use them for good." Gunda backed up Adowa.

"Our intentions are pure." Mahamba stood up and cleaned the dirt from his clothes.

"We still have some seeds but this time we will decide where to plant. We want to plant in Caputo ... it's a sacred place and it needs water and to be taken care of ... it will be mutually beneficial."

Adowa looked over to Gunda to confirm there were still seeds, and then to the forest.

"As you wish, madam."

Mahamba nodded and gave the orders to his leaders to follow Adowa's wishes.

"No, no leaders involved! Just us! You can hear us from Caputo, no need for supervision. You trust us, right?"

Adowa looked to the leaders' palace, since they had told us this fabricated story about hearing us. I still didn't buy it. I believed in the mystical power of Caputo, but I still didn't understand how they could hear us. Their house was the only house with a first floor, and it gave them enough of a view to see people coming. That was it.

"We are at your services madam Adowa." He kept the same sarcastic tone to seem controlled, but he was losing the battle. He didn't look so well. His eyes were heavy, swollen almost shut. He kept scratching them the whole time. First, I assumed it was the strong scent that came even from the dead plants, but it was something more, like his eyes were burning. Were the plants for him?

Adowa had always suffered from the disease of saying everything she thought. She couldn't control it and it rubbed people the wrong way, but now it was becoming handy. Growing up as a white girl, I had the privilege to be like that, to say whatever I thought, without consequences. People who suffer from this, they think that they owe the universe an explanation; they always need to be accountable and answer for all their thoughts.

Mahamba stopped the Babembas for a while, so we had Caputo

all to ourselves. I don't think they minded because the situation was getting out of hand. I heard Moxico say to Bengo that at the last Babemba a child had asked Mahamba 'what does opposition mean?' and he lost it. I didn't hear if he had answered or not, but that child was definitely a student of Adowa's and Harlow's lessons. They had to stop their teaching for now, but the Book was still being passed around till it reached all the families in the land. There was some kind of insurgency rising, and real hope would see the light of the day soon.

It was almost impossible to be there and not think about that day with Theo. I looked over at him and he was looking back at me with a naughty smile. The forest had our smell all over; we left our prints in the plants. I stepped back. I didn't want to enter the forest and start spoiling everything we did here, but we couldn't hide anymore, it was obvious that we were together, at least for now.

Gunda was testing the soil once again. He was more practical than Adowa. He believed in the recipe and how the herbs would be taking care of. Adowa was more into her intuition and kept declaring the usual things that we couldn't understand.

"People can't step on this area for a while," Gunda mumbled.

"We won't." I was still outside, afraid of what I was going to say if I entered.

"Let's plant around, not in the middle so they can still use the space for the Babembas while the plants are growing ... We don't want to interfere with their ruling."

Adowa rolled around like she was about to dance. I could sense she had a plan.

"We can't fail them again. Those are the last seeds," Theo whispered.

Could they hear us? I would rather not find out, so I stayed

164

behind watching them. They had already caught us for what the trees revealed. I didn't want to be another victim.

I watched them plant the plants, while I stayed in a corner. There were bugs everywhere. I could feel them close, and my body reacted. I felt something behind me. I smelled Namibe's familiar onion odor. He made a sign for me to follow him, and I did. I wanted to be away from the forest. I got away that day with Theo. I guess I had been overwhelmed with pleasure and won over by its mystical power, but one day it would catch me out, and I was afraid of what I was going to reveal. I hadn't seen Namibe since that day at the palace. I followed him and didn't ask questions. I hope they wouldn't notice I had gone.

We walked for hours. I had pain in my hunched back, tense from carrying my thoughts. I felt a strong punch in my bladder, and I could detect some kind of fluid slowly crawly down my legs. I wanted to tell him to stop somewhere, so I could go in between the plantation and check. Aunt Noli used to give me rags: sheep's wool and scraps from dresses, so I could use them to stem the flow. Most of us were so scared of the blacks for their mystical power but a woman could bleed for days without dying and they were not feared.

He took me to an area with piles of gray sand surrounding some kind of plantation. It looked like there were mini moun-tains of sand trying to cover up something. I heard different noises: from axes and something mechanical moving piles of rocks. There was a line of rails fixed to ties and laid on a roadbed, allowing for different containers to move. It was a track that led to a tunnel, smaller and darker than the tunnels in Rhodesia. Even though the white and black sides were crucified by each other, and the people feared each other, it was nothing compared to whatever was inside of that. Namibe didn't say a word, he just

165

watched me process everything. There were a lot of men, white, black, mixed, Benguela's tone, and even children, boys ... no signs of women, thank God! They all looked busy with allocated responsibilities.

I don't think I had ever seen gray sand before in my life. There was a lot of gray in Rhodesia to try to send the message of impartiality, but grey sand? The people were stepping on it and carrying that same sand from side to side. I kept seeing all kinds of men, even some with disabilities, probably caused by whatever they were doing there. I saw a black man with a huge derriere. Adowa told me about a land where black man had voluptuous bodies, because their mothers were curvy, and the genes were so strong. A long time ago, even before I was born, the whites would bring voluptuous women to our side to exhibit them as a freak show attraction. Only silly white men would find it funny to look at a curvy woman. I could think of many things to do with a woman like that. When Mom wanted to name me Sarah, Dad screamed and said 'no'. I guess he pictured me developing a big behind just like the infamous black woman Sarah Baartman from the land of Makhanda.

The blacks also had a mark on their arms, maybe cause by injections or an imprint from a certain tribe. They were all wearing boots that looked heavier than the feeling of Theo's body on top of me. I don't think I ever saw these faces, ever, where had they been the whole time? Were they kept here? I looked over to Namibe to see his reaction to what we were witnessing but he seemed like he already knew. The area was open, you could see the sky and it looked so near, like you could touch it. I kept studying the tunnels. They looked like caves. It felt like I had gone back in time. This was a bit different from any civilization I recognized. Like they created a new community

166

of people but at the same time they were using equipment that looked far ahead.

It smelled like something was burning, I looked down and the ground told me it was dying, just like Caputo. I was saw remains of trees; it seemed that they had completed erased what had been here before. I pictured them knocking down trees to create whatever was going on here. My brain refused to stop connecting the dots. The days we spent planting, and memories of physics class, allowed me to understand everything. I remember when Vince was fighting hard to add physics to our curriculum. Initially, the whites thought it was witchcraft because Vince kept talking about the sun, temperature range, soil type, and time then they realise that that it would be beneficial to the land to learn about it.

"A biome," I thought out loud.

"What?" Namibe asked, looking at me observing the people.

"Nothing. I am just trying to understand why you brought me." I didn't want to waste time explaining a biome but in the back of my mind, I could hear Vince preaching in class 'a distinct geographical region with specific climate and vegetation, that has formed in response to its physical environment and climate. A biome encompasses multiple ecosystems within its boundaries'. That's Elikya. I thought to myself, but this time silently.

"Keep looking ... You will understand."

"Who are all these people?"

"Those are mine workers."

"Mines? What are mines?"

I couldn't process anything. I saw waves of warmth, the sun was hotter than anything, I could feel the blood coming from my insides turn into crunchy remnants between my legs. This

167

was nothing like I ever seen. There was a heat mass engulfing these people. It was so hot that the sweat wouldn't last, it would automatically turn into something dry with a nasty smell.

"Those are mines, and the people here are mine workers."

I looked to what he pointed at, and it looked like a volcano erupted there. I don't think I ever saw a volcano, but I knew they existed somewhere, in some land.

"Where are we? Is this still Elikya?"

"Yes. We own this area. It was supposed to be a new area with houses for families."

"Deforestation." I kept thinking out loud. This time, he didn't hear me.

"He assigned us to be with you guys so we wouldn't interfere with his other plans." He looked at me to show that he hadn't had anything to do with this.

"Who else knows about this?" He ignored me and continued to describe the mines

"In that area where the sand has a more cream color ... It's for the gold."

I touched my necklace, I didn't know the process behind it.

"There used to be a river here, but they exploited it." He pointed at some area where a man was bowing down to do something in the ground.

"What are the hand bugs for?" I saw a few so I was wondering. We had used them to access groundwater, but it seemed they had another use here.

"For a lot of things. This is the exploration of the rock, which we call kimberlitic."

He told me in a way that meant I was focusing on the wrong things, but everything here seemed wrong.

"This is slavery." This didn't come from physics class; it came

168

from me.

"Yes ... and we need to do something about it!"

His eyes were red with rage; they looked sore. We just got the weakest link; Mahamba´s men were falling.

I walked as fast I could, I wanted to tell everyone what Mahamba had been doing to his own people. Namibe didn't stop me, he had a motive bringing me here, he knew he couldn't take him down alone, he needed the Rhodesian guts. I started running to avoid my dark thoughts: they took me back to everything I fought for years. There were handcuffs and shackles everywhere. These people were slaves! The elders from the black side still had marks from wearing cuffs when they were young. When Pastor Philips used to preach that we lived in peace, it meant that there was no longer slavery, they were no longer expressing their hate towards the blacks physically and aggressively, it had turned to just verbal aggression. Still, Vince wasn't convinced by that ceasefire where they still got away with everything they did to them.

My grandparents had owned slaves and deprived them of anything you can imagine. I don't remember growing up with slaves around the house, but Aunt Noli used to tell these stories about people helping mom cook and taking care of us.

As I walked, the weather was changing. I wasn't sure if it was going to rain or not. I just hoped it wasn't going to snow. These people wouldn't make it through the snow, just like I couldn't cope with my snowball of thoughts about colonization and racism all served in a banquet of hypocrisy. I left Namibe behind. He knew he had showed the situation to the right person, but I didn't know what to do with the information. I could only think about Harlow. It had taken her a lot to be vulnerable with me, and I had doubted her pain. How could I have ever doubted her? Mahamba was a monster!

"Where is Harlow?" I demanded to know as I entered the house.

Adowa, Theo and Gunda were around the table discussing a map. Adowa, with her authoritarian voice, was instructing them on what to do.

"She is in her room," Theo replied.

He tried to make a sign with his caring eyes; trying to ask me what was going on.

I spotted mugs on the table, and I thought about what I just saw. Whatever they were doing there, the water wouldn't be spared. Everything in this town was contaminated.

"Don't drink the water!"

When I shouted, Gunda and Adowa finally gave me attention, trying to understand why I was acting erratically. I left to find Harlow.

I carefully opened the door without making noise, I was inspecting the environment and how she was feeling. Harlow was sitting in bed, reading a book. She was wearing something that didn't hide her patches. She would only wear this at home. Harlow wasn't embarrassed of her patches; she just didn't want to rub any feathers. It took me time to understand it, but somewhere in people's weak minds they think that only physically perfect people are allowed to be proud, so they resort to shaming the appearance of others, talking about their skin, hair, and everything that makes up a person. Harlow was proud of her integrity and how she wasn't contaminated by others' thoughts.

"I need to talk to you." I had a will inside of me to let her know everything, but I didn't know what to say.

"Jodi." She closed the book and put it next to her. It was

170

probably one of the last books Benguela had stolen for her.

"What are you reading?" I was shaking but I still dared to sit on one corner of the bed. I understood how people feared her because she was a force.

"It's the diary of a child from my tribe. He was very short, so he was kept in a cage just like an animal and used as an attraction for public exhibition. He was humiliated and tortured. He was a slave."

When she said 'slave', the image of those people came to my mind.

"What was his name?"

"Ota. Pain seems like fiction until you experience it. Aren't you going to ask why him? What he did to deserve that? Do you think it was his fault?"

It was obvious that she was still upset about our last conversation. She mixed her disappointment towards me with her grief and was going to make me her punching bag. I was okay with that.

"Harlow, listen ... I am sorry."

I tried to get closer to her.

"I got the Book back. I think it went through the whole land ... I read it," she confessed.

I knew Elikyans had never read the Book before, including her.

"Growing up I was taught that all the holy stories were about white people ... and everything that was ill was referring to the blacks."

No matter how many years has passed, I still can't believe people in power could influence a whole land into believing that another group of people were not worthy.

"I'm not black or white, Jodi ... So where do I stand?"

She looked at her patches and wanted me to see them clearly.

171

She knew she was black, but she wanted me to pay for doubting her.

"I have something to tell you." I avoided eye contact with her because she was still upset. I wasn't sure what I was going to tell her. I had so many revelations. This one only came to me as I was walking back.

"I don't think Benguela's passing was natural." I spoke every word carefully; I didn't want to hurt her anymore. I wasn't sure about my suspicion, but I didn't want to have more secrets from her.

"What?" She seemed surprised.

"I remember seeing Benguela's eyes in the coffin ... they were reddish. She had an inflammation in her eyes caused by being exposed to dust and bacteria. I read about it...it's called 'red eye', it's viral and easily spread between people. Namibe told me that her last days were spent in their library. Their books are full of dust. She wanted to catch this. Some people sense when they are going to be killed, so they make sure they leave the killer with a mark."

"What are you saying, Jodi?" She stood up and started walking around the room.

"Benguela knew she was going to die."

"Mahamba is not a killer." She stopped walking around to face me, her eyes filling with tears.

"Harlow ... You know what he is capable of ... His eyes haven been swollen since the funeral."

"No ... No ... No ... Anyone who got close to her could catch it. It's a seasonal infection ... it comes and goes. A lot of people had it."

"Harlow, listen I have seen what he is capable of. He is constantly rubbing his eyes." I tried to hold her.

172

"No ... no ... he always had that. He has an issue with his eyes."
She stopped for a second and thought about it.

"Eye issue?"

"Yes. He always had that! When I lived with them, often Cabinda would take over to read on his behalf. He would complain about the size of the letters and with time his infection got worse." Hearing her defend him, I realized that she still cared for him.

"Cabinda?" I retorted. She had given me an idea. I don't think I bought her story about the eye infection or inflammation and whatever she used to defend her abuser. That's the thing about trauma, you fear the people who caused it. No matter how conceited Harlow seemed to most people, she was afraid of this man. She was still a child, like time stopped when her parents left her here. She had an armor of wisdom protecting her, but her inner child was still very much alive. She rested her head on my lap and told me that she hadn't been completely truthful. The reason why she had never stepped in to any Babembas to defend people she knew were being misjudged was because she was terrified of confessing that people's opinions did get to her and she didn't want them to know how it affected her. She refused to let them see her break; it was the only thing she still held on to.

She thanked me for the Book and said she had found solace in it. She fell asleep on my legs, just like Mirror used to. Her peaceful sleep showed that she had completely erased what I told her. Either she didn't want to believe that the man who raised her was a killer, or she felt I was overreacting.

The plants blossomed, strong and healthy. Adowa spoke to the plants with a very quiet voice, I don't know if it was part of her new mantra of speaking to the universe or if she was afraid that the leaders could hear her. She told Mahamba to wait, because they were not ready to be used yet. She then negotiated that Gunda's Babemba would take place first, and then they could collect the plants.

She was rehearsing how people were going to be organized in the space, in order to not destroy the dark plants. I watched proudly as all the leaders followed her directions.

Theo joined me in the grass, where I was being eating by all the bugs and living things beneath me, and the black flying insects harassing me.

"You have been busy."

Theo laughed at me struggling with the insects. I was in silence for a few minutes.

"I need to tell you something."

"Tell me ... yes, I will marry you," he joked.

Whatever plan Adowa had, it had put him and Gunda in the best mood.

"It's serious ... This land is not safe."

"What do you mean?"

"I mean that there's more than hunger. They are exploiting people. They are using them to extract diamonds and gold. The whole plan for feeding people wasn't for their sake; it was for the workers to be strong enough to work in the mines." I figured everything out in that exact moment.

"Who told you all this?" He didn't react how I was expecting. Instead, he resorted to playing with the grass.

"Why does it matter? I saw people working like slaves. Children! Children! You understand? They were wearing gloves - the gloves were dirty - there were cuffs everywhere Gigantic

174

pipes inside something like a tunnel, or a cave or a prison ... I don't know! There were huge rocks and wires inside of the cave. There was so many people. We gotta do something, Theo." I tried to explain it to him, drawing in the air with my hands. I couldn't control myself, maybe because it was that time of the month. Theo didn't say a word. You know when you keep repeating something to make people agree with you, but they are still not moved by it, that's how I felt.

"I already knew about everything, Jodi."

I never thought of Theo as a cold man, just practical. The weather was changing, just like Theo. Why couldn't people be charming forever? I couldn't bear to get to know this side of Theo. I wasn't ready to love another Vince.

"What do you mean you knew? And you never said anything??? Theo, there are children in danger ... they were carrying heavy things." You know when you are disrespected, and you ask again what people said to see if they would dare to disrespect you. I pleaded with him for some kind of sympathy.

"I don't care Jodi ... I only care about you ... Caleb ... Mirror."

He was basically saying 'I love you' but it didn't land like that.

"And Mariane?" I opened my mouth wide; I wanted him to hear me clearly. This was uncalled for, but it was the only response I could think of to so much indifference.

"I have lost you once ... I don't want to lose you again ... I don't have time to waste ... This is not our battle ... We don't owe these people anything."

I started scratching my head like I had lice, I scratched with so much anger that it probably wounded my scalp.

"This is really how you feel ... Huh." I could feel my heart fighting a heart attack. This took me back to years ago when he came to my house to say that he was going to marry Mariane.

I needed to be away from him for a while. I just couldn't believe he became this frigid, like a mild version of Vince. What happens in people's lives that completely changes them? Losing my mother, my sister, the father of my child, and respect for my own father, didn't change me to the point to not care about others, no matter how much I wish I didn't.

I left him there; I didn't want him to see me cry. I thought Theo was the only man I could show vulnerability to, but I was wrong. I have flashbacks of Vince calling me weak, and my body shudders every time I think about it. I wanted to throw things, but I wasn't a spoiled little white girl anymore who had her own room and things to throw. Back then, things really didn't me upset me, there was nothing to be angry about, I didn't care about how black teachers were treated in school, I didn't care about the horrific stories I heard about what my people did to them. I just didn't care. My character has developed to be more empathetic, while others have become the opposite.

Theo waited for me to calm down before sharing what he really knew. I hate when men say that we need to calm down, especially in the sacred days, like being in this phase makes us unbalanced. That was a form of manipulation that I couldn't stand from any man.

On the black side, when a woman was on her period, she couldn't do anything, and she was kept isolated. She couldn't touch the food and her food was separated from the others. They saw it as a way to respect her body, but I saw it as abuse. I wonder how would you know when someone was on their period? How could information like that be shared in a community? I was spared from this traditional act because I basically joined them when

I already had Mirror and that gave me some kind of immunity towards all those rules. I always thought we the whites had many rules and laws, but the blacks were so bureaucratic, conventional and restrained. So many directives for funerals, weddings, birthdays, rites of passage and the likes. I couldn't stand it! And I couldn't complain because all of the white side hated me, so I didn't have anywhere to go for shelter and protection, except to Aunt Noli.

Theo later revealed that when we were on the farms, when Moxico would bring us water, he had noticed his shoes were dirty with dark sand, different than the red sand in town or the brown on the farm. I don't remember that at all, I was just too busy fighting insects. He had spotted this several times and he wondered about it. He shared that he heard about a land that was extracting minerals from the earth, but he didn't know it was Elikya. He was familiar with everything I described and explained the automation of the underground mine ventilation system and how it helped to keep oxygen in the mine. His car had a similar ventilation system but for another purpose. I was glad that at least people there were able to breathe, but no one could convince me that place was safe for a child.

I decided to meet Cabinda, maybe the opposition that kid mentioned, was being formed within the leaders.

"I wasn't expecting you Miss Collins." Cabinda claimed this, but his body language showed he wasn't surprised.

"Who were you expecting?" I tried to make my voice raspy and strong, to make him fear me or something.

"I don't know. We, the leaders, are often asked to meet with the people. Namibe didn't tell me who." He walked a bit, showing his arrogant gait and his pride in being one of the leaders.

"I know. You guys are really fighting for your people." I followed his eyes with my sarcastic ones.

"We try our best." He smiled but it was so vain. He was one of the leaders who really enjoyed his status and not his responsibilities, and one of those who Mahamba trusted the most.

"Cabinda ... You know what he is doing. Look at this place, he is exploiting this land. The land is dying. The people need you."

"'Dirty water doesn't stop plants from growing' There are always going to be problems Jodi..." He held one of the branches of the tree, maybe to keep his balance and the equilibrium of his lies.

"I don't care about those useless analogies that he reads to you ... He is so controlling to the point that he even reads *to* you, like he wants to control your thoughts and ideologies ... that man is a dictator!!!" I got closer to him.

"He doesn't read to us ... He lets me take over and read for the others ... He trusts me ... You don't know anything ... You think you know ... He is a good man who cares for his people ... He has done so much for me and my family." He held my neck like he was about to choke me. He said something that activated a light in my brain, but I wasn't sure if I could trust my instincts. People love to frame you as naïve and innocent, claiming that there is something that we don't know, when in reality they are the clueless ones.

"He wants to control everything! He wants the mines ... The dark plants ... He is greedy ... He wants everything!!! ... Why would he want the dark plants?!! He starves his people and then wants to heal them? You can't take medicine without food ... You can't fully heal with an empty stomach ... I find that hard to believe."

I held the tree to steady myself and escape Cabinda's grasp. It hurt, but I had to endure. I felt my blood vessels struggling to find oxygen like they were stuck in the mines.

"The dark plants are for me. My child is sick. He is doing that for my family."

The thin skin of his eyelids were inflamed with pain. He released my neck from his scarred hands. I didn't know much about the leader's family; it was hard enough to memorize all of them.

"I am sorry ... But what about Benguela? You know he had something to do with her death. He found out she was helping us teach children how to read and he wanted to chastise us." My voice was horse after he had almost strangled me.

"Hmm. It was very unfortunate what happened to her, she went through a lot ... She is now resting." His painful eyes changed to red.

"Unfortunate? You know he has something to do with that."

"You know Jodi, tragedies come in pairs."

He ended the conversation, while slowly walking away, heading back to the village. I hated threats! What was he implying? That another death was coming?? I couldn't stand these people and their menaces disguised in figure of speech.

Chapter 10

I woke up to the sound of drums and other instruments as well as the sound of people marching with a lot more stamina than usual. The atmosphere was happy. I wasn't sure what they were celebrating, but I didn't expect much from people who cheered when they were told they were not going to eat for 40 days.

Adowa was helping Gunda get ready. She was saying her affirmations, and he repeated them with conviction, 'I am a good man', 'I am a child of THEY', 'Everything is going to be okay'. I believed in her new self-discovered Zen and positive self, but I also believed they had a trick up their sleeves, in spite of the sleeveless attire they were wearing, given to them by Mahamba. I refused to wear the outfits; Harlow's pride had influenced me.

We all walked in the direction of Caputo. There were a lot of people; I had never seen that many people. I didn't think that the village had space for all of those people. Harlow told me that people had arrived to support their relatives who had been kept incarcerated for years and never given a proper Babemba. I saw the Habesha women who came from the Abyssinia land, a land known for having the most beautiful women. They had a dirty water tone, but they were shiny like they were covered by a sacred fruit oil.

I finally saw the mixed people I came here to see, the people who were a perfect end result of a white and black race relations, with no patches, no lack of pigment or anything, just *mulattos*...I saw a lot of kinky hair – like sponges; I could wash my body with that hair. It made me think about Mirror's hair and how strong it was. I would rely on Adowa to braid him because I couldn't cope. She would place him between her legs and plait his curly and thick hair, a result of the shape of his hair follicles. In the back of my freak my mind, I always wondered if he would get turned on by the fishy but pleasant smell of a woman's private parts so close to him. I didn't mind my son liking women, I heard about men who didn't like woman and how crucified they were for being different. I didn't wish that for my son;, he was had already been born with a lot on his plate.

Namibe, Cunene, and Huila were instructing people where to stand. They indicated that we should all stand on one side of the forest and on the parallel side were the leaders. We were all standing around the forest like we were fences trying to protect it. Theo held my hand like he was afraid something was going to happen; I don't think he completely knew Adowa's plan. I don't think anyone knew, not even Gunda. Probably only Kofi knew. Yes, Gunda's fate was dependent on a 'dark skin man with a bag', as Adowa described him.

Gunda was ready to enter Caputo, when Harlow stopped him and whispered in his ear. I read her lips and saw that she said, "Trust the birds."

I wondered what it meant.

Theo inspected my neck and before he could say something about the bruising, we heard them calling Gunda to the center so that the Babemba could start.

"We are gathered today to welcome Gunda to our land."

Mahamba repeated those same words I was getting accustomed to.

"My name is Mahamba, I am the main leader of Elikya ... the land of hope. Years ago, we decided to create a way to protect our land from ill-intentioned guests."

Listening to this after all we went through in this land didn't taste the same.

"I want to introduce you the leaders ... Luanda, Cabinda, Bie, Bengo, Lunda-Sul, Lunda-Norte, Kuanza Norte, Kuanza Sul, Namibe, Uige, Zaire, Huila, Huambo, Cuando-Cubango, Cunene, Malanje and Moxico ... They are all here for you."

It was more apparent that Benguela was absent when he said all their names. I wondered if she was going to be replaced, because now they were no longer even. I also thought about Cabinda's threat, and I shivered.

"Gunda please tell us why you are here."

Mahamba always had his head high, and I reflected about Namibe saying, 'Reading is humility'. I kept repeating it. I knew there was a message behind that, but I couldn't figure out yet what it was, but I knew I was about to. The truth seemed so near, but I couldn't reach it. It felt like struggling to reach an orgasm.

"My name is Gunda ... I came from Rhodesia ... A land that was divided. We fought very hard to end that segregation but that fighting cost us a lot. It cost us the lives of our loved ones. But we also took the lives of the loved ones of other people."

There was a murmur of disappointment in the crowd.

"I killed a man who was just taking orders ... it wasn't his fault ... he was injecting people with a substance that he was told wouldn't do any harm. I don't think he wanted to harm us, but he did. It killed my father. I loved my father. I would do anything to be with him again. Losing my father was like losing my purpose in life. My father was the only thing keeping me alive."

If prison is indeed the place for redemption, he was a good example of it.

"Then I found another reason to live. I was serving my sentence in my land, when I was saved by love, a love I never knew I could feel, that I never knew I would be deserving of ... Then I lost it."

The whole crowed gasped.

"The thing about grief is that it has no cure, you can't do anything about it, it's just there ... You just need to accept it. Grief is my sentence so I am at your mercy, sir. Whatever you decide." He bowed to his knees, but I suspected that he was giving a sign to Adowa because why would Gunda be so subservient to Mahamba?

I saw Adowa walking very fast, like a shadow, and going to where the leaders were standing. I looked to Harlow to see if she caught something. She didn't. She was in her thoughts, probably thinking about her late friend.

"Harlow, what is Mahamba's favorite book?" I asked in a very low voice.

I didn't think it was the best moment, but something was eating me.

"A green one."

"What's the title?"

I looked around to see if anyone could hear us, but everyone was busy watching the leaders have their talk or talking between themselves.

"I can't remember. He would always ask 'for the green book'."

While the leaders were making their deliberations, I looked around to see if anyone would say something. It was the time for someone to step up, but no one ever did. Harlow took a step ahead to enter the circle. I stopped her because she didn't have to sacrifice her peace of mind because of Gunda. If people can be influenced to hate you for no reason, imagine what they will do to you if they find out your weaknesses.

I wasn't sure what the plan was, but the last few days I had eavesdropped something here and there, and I knew I could trust Adowa. I looked over to my left side to see where Theo was, and he was nowhere to be found. I saw some commotion, something was happening.

Theo was running and Adowa too, Harlow was still next to me.

The crowd was getting impatient and were making a fuss. It was so crowded that I could smell everyone's funky smell, like burnt hair. A smell of maize came in from the farms to ease my nostril. I had a fleeting thought that the maize was finally growing.

I tried to follow Adowa with my eyes and could track her for a moment, but then she would disappear, so I tried to concentrate on Theo. I saw him pushing Luanda to beyond the trees, close to the center. Then I saw Adowa doing the same to Cabinda, Bié, Bengo, Lunda-Sul, Lunda-Norte, Kuanza Norte, Kuanza Sul, in that order. She was aggressive and fast. The leaders were screaming, and all looked puzzled. Then Theo pushed Uige, Zaire, Huambo, Cuando-Cubango, and Moxico. Namibe pushed Malanje, then Huìla pushed Huambo.

I didn't have time to think so I moved my body with a new so-called strength raised from fasting and pushed Mahamba.

The leaders tried to go back and hide in trees where they usually stood but the ground started to shake, like it was announcing a volcano. Stems were growing in the ground, but they were full of rage, and they crawled beneath each of the leaders' feet and ambushed them. Anywhere they put their feet, buds, petioles, axils, and internodes were growing to stop them from moving. I had watched the plants in the farm slowly growing for weeks, but these plants were different. The leaders tried to shake them away, and jiggle them off, but they were stubborn. The plants danced around their legs like snakes.

"What is this?" Mahamba shouted as he pulled up his attire to check what was underneath.

"Don't move. They are mines," Bengo warned Mahamba, making gestures with his arms.

"Landmines?"

Cabinda looked down to study them.

"No ... They are plans. Carnivorous plants," Lunda-Sul said, while avoiding looking down like she was scared of what was holding her.

"It's dark plants!" Kuanza Norte said, as she bent to study them.

"They are deadly!" Lunda-Norte was calmer than others, but she knew their fate. "Whenever we are distributing food, I ... I ... I ... remove ... remove ... a few names from the list ... because they don't give me the respect I deserve!!!"

The mystical power was finally kicking in. Gunda stood up to watch them get beaten by their own poison. He was holding his anger, and his veins became red, just like his eyes.

"I don't care for these people. I only care about myself," Malanje owned up.

"There are people who wanted to be leaders and had good

intentions ... Genuine ones ... But I made sure they didn't stand a chance. I lied about them. I told Mahamba they were not a good fit," Zaire confessed.

"I wanted to change this land ... I wanted to be a leader for a good cause, but power went through my head ... I forgot my people ... My family." Uige closed his eyes with shame.

"I wasn't like this ... I wanted to do good ... but I was weak ... I was told that if you wanted to be a leader you needed to kill your own son and I did ... I poisoned my son, but he didn't die. He is sick and he will never have a normal life." Cabinda fought his own words, while tears poured down his red eyes. I looked around trying to see if his family was around, but gladly they were nowhere to be found.

"I sold my daughter to become a leader." Bié kept kicking the plants, but they had already got out what they wanted.

"I have recruited people to go to the mines, in exchange for food. They have worked days and nights. The people are tired. Every single day they work like slaves for just a piece of bread. I don't give them anything ... just false promises." Moxico admitted.

"Kwanza Sul is a good leader. She cares for people. She wants to do good. I am not. I made sure Mahamba didn't see her good deeds. I took credit for many of them. I alienated her from all the leaders. I lied about her many times," Lunda-Sul confessed while looking at Kwanza-Sul.

"We all had good intentions when we joined but now whenever Mahamba wants to add a new leader with the ambition to do good, we convince him not to. We paint him in a bad light. We don't want them to interfere with what we are doing. We keep the food for ourselves but we are lazy. We don't want to grow the harvest. We want others to serve us, but we don't feed them

186

enough for them to have the stamina to plant. Bad emanations. We deserved years of drought because we made a drought out of these people's lives."

Kwanza Sul kept looking at the crowd, asking forgiveness with his hands.

People froze, they didn't know what to do with the information, they were beginning to realize all the things they had suffered. In a way, being deprived of knowledge had blinded them but it had saved them from hating themselves and their situation.

I looked up and saw a few holy green leaves slowly changing to a dry brown; they were falling. The more the trees heard, the more they died. There was a shower of parched leaves. They were lifeless and lightweight; you could barely feel them.

"I suggested sending children to work in the mines. We needed to increase human capacity. There weren't enough men, so I suggested children. We lost many of them in accidents that could have been avoided," Cuando-Cubango confessed in a guilty voice.

Did the forest also influence their self-awareness? They seemed to know what they did and how ill it was. I used to think that people like this were not aware of their actions because they used to preach and brag about their deeds, like they lived in their own bubble of hypocrisy.

"I told Mahamba that Benguela was stealing books to give to Harlow and the Rhodesians. I felt bad but still I didn't have the courage to confess so I told Namibe about the mines because I knew he was going to do something about it." Huila entered the pack; she didn't wait till the plants circled her. When she mentioned Benguela, tears fell from her red eyes.

"We have watched all these unfold but we are weak, we fear

for our families. I learned about the mines, but I was not brave enough to stand against Mahamba. I hoped Jodi would. do something about it. I know what we are doing is wrong, but I kept quiet." Namibe followed Huila and didn't hesitate, he didn't fight the power of the forest.

"We don't admire Mahamba. I don't think he is clever. He is not smart. He is not intelligent. He is a fool … a puppet … Me and Cabinda are plotting against him … We will kill him when we have a chance." Huambo shocked us all.

We all looked at Mahamba to see his reaction, he was mumbling something, still fighting the plants and the power of Caputo.

"I know the leaders don't have the best interest of the people at heart. They don't care about them … I always knew … but I pretended I believed in the cause so I could join them … because we all have to comprise our beliefs to have some kind of prosperity in life."

We had to follow his voice because at some point, they had begun speaking at the same time.

Cunene looked at the crowd, trying to convince us that it was how life should be. He expressed the mantra of the corrupted. They think that's the only way, that you need to be close to those people to get further in life. Little do they know that if they kept being themselves, and keep their character untouched, it would take them to further places. They rather comply to the hypocrisy and oppression, slowly embodying them. 'if you swim in pollution, you get polluted'. This echoed in my mind, I knew I had heard it before. I knew it came from one of Vince's idols, the leaders he aspired to be, leaders with integrity, the opposite of these ones.

"I always thought my family was doing good for the people

Elikya, so I wanted to do good too but I wasn't a very clever child. I struggled my whole life. I am illiterate, so I made sure the next generation after me, didn't know how to read. I created the reading sessions with the leaders so I could drink from their wisdom and listen to the readings. I miss Harlow reading to me." Mahamba looked at her like she was something precious, his red eyes filled with nostalgia.

"I always wanted to have a family, so I raised Harlow like my own. She was smart and fearful, everything I aspired to be but when she disobeyed me, I had no option than to completely estrange her from the land. She didn't deserve that. Power got to me, and I couldn't stand anyone who would go against me. I then realized I could get more power with more possessions. So everything became a source of power and self-entitlement. When I found the mines, I wanted the coal, the gold, and the iron ore. I had a dream that if I possessed them all, I could hear everything in this land. Not only in Caputo but anywhere. I could feel that people were scheming against me, to take me out of power, so I wanted to make sure I knew who."

Mahamba bowed down, with the plants all over his legs. I had realized that Mahamba was illiterate because his arrogance never allowed him to have his head down, and Namibe's remark kept pounding in my brain 'reading is humility'.

"I am sorry my people. I starved you for years because I needed to have control and servitude. I needed you to need me." His arrogant voice suddenly became soft.

There was silence. No one dared to say anything.

I spotted the gypsy lady. I carefully got close to her, sliding myself between the people, and I finally pushed her, touching her hair laying along her back. She was flabbergasted, trying to understand why I pushed her. Her surprised eyes instantly focused on Harlow like she was going to scapegoat her again. She kept looking at her, trying to get answers, and seeing Harlow's angelic face triggered her to say exactly what I wanted her to.

"Harlow has been nothing but good to me and my family. She has helped me so much more than anyone in this town. When my son was sick she gave us food. She is a good woman ... I ... I ... I ... I went through a lot ... I became angry and I diverted my anger towards the one person who was helping me because I knew she was a genuinely good person and wasn't going to retaliate to whatever I did to her. I was tired of this system ... leaders and more leaders but no change. I knew I couldn't complain because I knew they could do something to me. So I found my punching bag ... Harlow ... Harlow is a saint ... she should be the only and one leader."

She had her knees on the ground and curled them to ease the painful rigidity. She never stop looking at Harlow. The plants hadn't even touched her, she knew it was her chance to redeem herself. The crowd started screaming 'ungrateful', the same word they used to drag Harlow, the same label they used to destroy her life.

These people were so easily influenced by whatever they were told.

Vince once told me about a land called Cazenga, and whenever they saw somebody beating up someone, random people would join, without asking questions, till they killed the person. They did the same to Harlow, no questions asked, they just destroyed her to see how much she could take.

"I feel sorry for you." Adowa stepped in and addressed the gypsy lady. She then turned to the leaders.

"You have done enough. But more than what you did to these people. You have sacrificed your own land for power. Changes in temperatures and the lack of trees cause soil erosion. The ecosystem must be respected, each animal has its function in nature ... the chances of food shortages will be high ... You can't do something to the earth and not be accountable to ... 'if you swim in pollution, you get polluted'."

Adowa spoke like a true mother of the land, like the Zen queen she was slowly becoming. Her voice had changed from always angry to peaceful and serene, the kind of voice that you wanted to hear from, learn from ... She exuded a one-of-a-kind powerful energy. She gazed at me and gave me a wink. Was her power back? Had she read my mind?

"Feeding people on the floor and throwing crumbs is not feeding people. You have all treated your people like you are doing them a favor. Treating them as less than human."

Gunda finally stood up and addressed his judging committee. I almost forgot about him and his Babemba. Harlow was right, this was not about him at all, Gunda had just been a distraction.

"They always complain. They are ungrateful. 'If external approval is your only source of food, you'll be hungry forever'," the annoying Cabinda intervened. They loved to quote things that they did not understand.

Harlow carefully entered the circle, each step she took made our hearts beat faster.

"Just like you made the people hungry forever. People will always complain indeed, and they are ungrateful indeed. They will go against the only person that will give them a hand." She looked at the gypsy lady but instead of pushing her down, she gave her a hand to stand up.

"But if we live our lives caring about possessions it will slowly ruin our spirit, deprive us of peace, and we will become victims of blind greed and uncontrollable forces. I have loved this land

191

in ways that it could never love me back, but I still have hope and hope keeps us going ... I am hope ... You are hope."

She gracefully pointed at each person in the crowd. They all entered the space and held her like she was the queen of Elikya. That was Harlow's fairy tale, the grace and the respect she deserved. I kept looking at her, trying to understand her force. Who was she? Who gave her so much integrity? How could she have so much faith without ever reading the Book? I kept looking at her, mesmerized by her strength.

The prison guards appeared from nowhere, as though the forest called them through telepathy. They took the leaders, one by one, with their swollen red eyes, and helped them to escape from the grip of the almighty dark plants.

Some of them tried to fight the guards and use their arrogance to intimidate them. Others were consumed by shame and accepted their fate. But none of them (all with red swollen and suspicious eyes) came forward with what happened to Benguela. Perhaps she had succumbed to her condition. I realized that at some point I was also suffering from 'red eye', and it might have spread to others. My allergy to animal hair and animosity toward nature itself was also a trigger.

The leaders held Harlow up and claimed her as the new and only leader, ending the years of oppression by the eighteen chosen ones.

I heard the familiar sound of an engine getting closer. I saw a red car coming towards us. It was Theo's car.

"Mom!!!!" a mixed boy screamed. I hadn't been called that name for months.

"Mirror?!." I wasn't sure if it was him. I kept walking towards

192

the child.

Theo came towards me.

"Mom ... mom ... mom." He looked older but hearing his soft voice calling me Mom made him seem like a toddler.

"Mirror ... my baby."

I used to make him blush when I called him that. I hugged him so strong till I felt his newly toned arms melt into my love. I was glad that the elder women from the black side had allowed me to breastfeed him longer to make him stronger. If he had been born a girl, they wouldn't have let me. He smelled like Aunt Noli but with a sprinkle of the ocean. I peeked a bit under his shirt, and I noticed that his patches were more scattered.

I looked up and noticed that there were other people with him – Caleb and a white girl.

"Mom ... We had to come ... We were worried about you."

"I was worried about you too. I am sorry. So much has happened here, but I knew I left you in good hands."

I unlocked from the hug, and I stared at him, inspecting his face to understand his reaction to what I said.

I looked over to Caleb and the girl to see if they would give anything away, but they were stiff. A minute ago, they were smiling and happy to see me but then they seemed to completely turn off their emotions. The moment turned into an emotionally charged situation. I wanted to call Adowa to tell me what she could sense because no one was saying anything. Theo was busy hugging and catching up with Caleb, who also seemed to have some disturbing news.

"What happened?" I turned my head side to side, trying to read Mirror. He raised his eyebrows, lowered the corners of his small mouth, and his posture slumped. Then Mirror turned to Theo, like he was asking for help.

"Mom ... Aunt Noli," Mirror mumbled with his head down.

"What about Aunt Noli? What??!!!" I started shaking him and then looking over to Theo for some kind of answer.

"She passed away a few months ago ... I am really sorry, Mom." He held his head up to face me and give me his condolences, and, in a way, to apologize for mistreating her in the past. Based on Mirror's voice, in the time he had spent with her he had grown to love her and understand the amazing woman she was. Had been! I corrected in my mind.

"No ... no ... no ... no ... No!!!!" I started screaming like a maniac. I saw Adowa and Gunda approaching to understand what had happened, but I didn't want to speak to them and have to explain what kind of woman my aunt was. To them, she was just a white lady, to me, she was everything.

I started running and running, I wanted to be left alone. I didn't want to think about what to say to not hurt anyone, or to strategize my words to protect people, I just wanted to be alone for a few hours. I ran like I had not run in eyes, the kind of running that forces your bones so that you release any pain you have or lingering feeling, like you want to challenge your sore muscles, muscles that are stuck, until you finally release them to their full potential. I lost my shoes on the way. I was running barefoot, stepping into the different types of sands in this traumatized land, the victim of human hands.

It felt good, Adowa was right. Walking barefoot on the white side was a daring and disrespectful move to your family and society while on the black side, it was just a way to connect to earth. She told me it stimulates blood circulation and improves tissue oxygenation, the oxygen the Caputo trees needed. The feet are the anchor for the body and my aunt was my anchor.

I found myself under the sacred tree, the shadow of the

branches protecting me from my rain of grief. I lost track of time, but my mind felt tranquil after running.

Harlow once said that 'grief is wisdom and wisdom is protection' but I didn't feel protected at all. Having someone you love alive was an assurance that everything was going to be okay. It was like believing in good amid despair. I thought about things in another light. In the mines, there were always stars in the sky. In the drought, the people were happy, dancing, celebrating; the warmth of the people brought them together. In the hunger, you learned to be grateful for a meal when you had it; you practiced self-control and mastered fasting, which helped us to grow in our faith. We enjoy the good times, but they don't last. In the bad times, we learn. And in between, we live.

I wished I could go back and pause a moment with her, a happy moment where I was trying on a new dress she made or digesting a lesson she shared. I wanted to pause the moment and send a message to my older self; to enjoy it and pin the moment so I wouldn't forget nor take it for granted. I wish I had known...

"Mom." Mirror showed up and woke me from my thoughts of grief. I could feel that there was something more, but I was afraid of asking. I couldn't bear anything else. My aunt was dead!

"I am okay, Mirror."

I started cleaning my tears from my swollen face by roughly passing my hands over my skin. That's the thing I didn't like about being a mother – I always had to be strong, to put a façade.

"It's okay, Mom. You don't need to be strong for me." He sat down next to me.

"She was one of a kind, Mirror. I wish you knew how good she was." My tears joined my smile, like an unexpected sunset.

"I know, Mom ... I spent her last days with her, and I understand you. She was good a woman just like you. Just like Nicola."

He wasn't trying to make Aunt Noli seem like a regular loss; he was trying to introduce the subject that Nicola had passed. And I could feel that he wanted a hug.

"Nicola? What about Nicola, Mirror?!" I already knew in my heart, but I needed to be sure.

"Nicola is gone, Mom." He squinted his eyes and started crying like the baby he was, the baby I never took care of and gave to the blacks. I held him in my arms like he wasn't this well-built man with a body just like his dad. He cried and sobbed like a soulless person with a soul. I finally felt like a real mother, I could feel that he longed for my hug to finally end his mourning.

Before Adowa and Gunda returned to Rhodesia, she called everyone to join her at Caputo's vigil. She taught us the power of positive thinking, the value of meditation, and she asked us to stand around the forest in a chain formation to speak positive affirmations around it. She instructed us on how to perform breathing exercises, and bodily postures, for health and relaxation. She told us to repeat after her 'Caputo is sacred ... Caputo is powerful ... We are part of the natural world, and I am grateful to live, breathe, walk, and play on this beautiful planet that I get to call home'.

We could feel something in the air changing.

I held Theo's hand and gazed at him saying with my eyes that I loved him, and I forgave him for not telling me my aunt had passed. I knew he had just wanted to protect me like always.

We did the same at the farms, where people had the free will to plant now, and Harlow was in charge of helping them divide the areas for each family to claim, so everyone could rely on the harvest. Children were not allowed to be anywhere near the mines. The operation continued but only strong men with the passion for mining were allowed to work – at a reasonable time, with proper breaks, with good nutrition and adequate compensation.

Harlow ordered that the crystals found in the mines be used for spiritual and mental exercises. They were all different minerals. They had an eccentric appearance. Some were clear like a crystal ball where you could see the future, and, somehow you could, if you believed, just like Adowa taught us. Others were like small boulders with skewered pieces. The crystals helped the community in many ways, with mental and physical healing, the healing Mahamba claimed he was looking for.

With the same gems they polished them to make tempered glass to make a community kitchen, a place where food was given to all the people freely, to completely end hunger in Elikya.

We heard the Babembas of each leader. Whatever their fates were, we didn't care, we were focusing on ours, and on building a home here for our family.

The END

"The forest was shrinking, but the trees kept voting for the axe, because its handle was wooden, and they thought it was one of them." Turkish proverb.

Made in the USA
Monee, IL
13 June 2025

18114649R00121